S0-BZE-018

YASHAR KEMAL

Günesh Karabuda

Yashar in an old quarter of Istanbul, with the Genoese tower of Galata in the background, a landmark of the city.

Yashar Kemal was born in 1922 in the small village of Hemite in the cotton-growing plains of Southern Anatolia. His father's family were feudal lords, his mother's, brigands. At the age of five, Kemal saw his father murdered in a Mosque. The shock caused him to develop a stammer, and for several years he was only free from it when he sang. As a result, he began to improvise songs in the tradition of the Anatolian minstrels.

When he was nine, Kemal decided to learn to read and write. He had to walk daily to a distant village to do so and eventually he went for three years to a secondary school at Adana. He then worked in the local rice and cotton fields, operated a threshing machine and became a factory worker. As champion of landless peasants, he was hounded out of every job.

Yet he managed to save enough money to buy a typewriter and set himself up as a public letter writer in the small town of Kadirli. Later he went to Istanbul and became a reporter. In 1952 he published a book of short stories and in 1955 came his first novel, Memed my Hawk. This book won the best novel of the year prize in Turkey and its hero has since become a living legend among the peasants of Anatolia.

Yashar Kemal is now considered the greatest living Turkish writer. His books have been translated into many languages and he has been discussed as a future Nobel Prize winner.

Yashar Kemal was a member of the Central Committee of the Turkish Workers' Party, now banned.

Other fiction by
YASHAR KEMAL

Memel My Hawk

They Burn the Thistles (Memel My Hawk, Part II)

The Wind from the Plain

Anatolian Tales

Iron Earth, Copper Sky

The Legend of Ararat

The Legend of the Thousand Bulls

The Undying Grass

The Lords of Akchasaz

Seagull

ANATOLIAN TALES

YASHAR KEMAL

TRANSLATED FROM THE TURKISH

BY THILDA KEMAL

Writers and Readers

London   New York

Writers and Readers Publishing Cooperative Society Ltd.
144 Camden High Street, London NW1 0NE, England

Published by Writers and Readers Publishing
Cooperative Society Ltd. 1983

Copyright © 1968 Yashar Kemal
Copyright © 1968 in the English translation by
William Collins Sons & Co Ltd., London

All Rights Reserved

Printed at the University Press, Oxford

This book is sold subject to the condition that it shall not, by way
of trade or otherwise, be lent, re-sold, hired out, or otherwise
circulated without the publisher's prior consent in any form of
binding or cover other than that in which it is published and
without a similar condition including this condition being
imposed on the subsequent purchaser

CONTENTS

A Dirty Story

The three of them were sitting on the damp earth, their backs against the dung-daubed brush-wall and their knees drawn up to their chests, when another man walked up and crouched beside them.

'Have you heard?' said one of them excitedly. 'Broken-Nose Jabbar's done it again! You know Jabbar, the fellow who brings all those women from the mountain villages and sells them in the plain? Well, this time he's come down with a couple of real beauties. The lads of Misdik have got together and bought one of them on the spot, and now they're having fun and making her dance and all that . . . It's unbelievable! Where does the fellow find so many women? How does he get them to come with him? He's the devil's own son, he is . . .'

'Well, that's how he makes a living,' commented one of the men. 'Ever since I can remember, this Jabbar's been peddling women for the villagers of the Chukurova plain. Allah provides for all and sundry . . .'

'He's still got the other one,' said the newcomer, 'and he's ready to give her away for a hundred liras.'

'He'll find a customer soon enough,' put in another man whose head was hunched between his shoulders. 'A good woman's worth more than a team of oxen, at least, in the Chukurova plain she is. You can always put her to the plough and, come summer, she'll bind and carry the sheaves, hoe, do anything. What's a hundred liras? Why, a woman

7

brings in that much in one single summer. In the fields, at
home, in bed. There's nothing like a woman. What's a
hundred liras?'

Just then, Hollow Osman came up mumbling to himself
and flopped down beside them without a word of greeting.
He was a tall, broad-shouldered man with a rather shapeless
pot-bellied body. His lips drooped foolishly and his eyes
had an odd squint-like gaze.

'Hey, Osman,' the man who had been talking addressed
him. 'Broken-Nose Jabbar's got a woman for sale again.
Only a hundred liras. Tell Mistress Huru to buy her for
you and have done with living alone and sleeping in barns
like a dog.'

Osman shrugged his shoulders doubtfully.

'Look here, man,' pursued the other, 'this is a chance in a
million. What's a hundred liras? You've been slaving for
that Huru since you dropped out of your mother's womb
and she's never paid you a lira. She owes you this. And
anyway she'll get back her money's worth in just one summer.
A woman's good for everything, in the house, in the fields,
in bed . . .'

Osman rose abruptly.

'I'll ask the Mistress,' he said. 'How should I know? . . .'

A couple of days later, a short, broad-hipped girl with blue
beads strung into her plaited hair was seen at the door of
Huru's barn in which Hollow Osman always slept. She was
staring out with huge wondering eyes.

A month passed. Two months . . . And passers-by grew
familiar with the sight of the strange wide-eyed girl at the
barn door.

One day, a small dark boy with a face the size of a hand
was seen pelting through the village. He rushed up to his

mother where she sat on the threshold of her hut gossiping with Seedy Doneh.

'Mother,' he screeched, 'I've seen them! It's the truth, I swear it is. Uncle Osman's wife with . . . May my eyes drop out right here if I'm telling a lie.'

Seedy Doneh turned to him sharply.

'What?' she cried. 'Say it again. What's that about Fadik?'

'She was with the Agha's son. I saw them with my own eyes. He went into the barn with her. They couldn't see me where I was hiding. Then he took off his boots, you know the shiny yellow boots he wears . . . And then they lay down and . . . Let my two eyes drop out if . . .'

'I knew it!' crowed Seedy Doneh. 'I knew it would turn out this way.'

'Hollow Osman never had any manhood in him anyway,' said the child's mother. 'Always under that viper-tongued Huru's petticoats . . .'

'Didn't I tell you, Ansha, the very first day she came here that this would happen?' said Doneh. 'I said this girl's ready to play around. Pretending she was too bashful to speak to anyone. Ah, still waters run deep . . .'

She rose quickly and hurried off to spread the news.

'Have you heard? Just as I foretold . . . Still waters . . . The Agha's son . . . Fadik . . .'

In a trice all the neighbouring women had crowded at Ansha's door, trying to squeeze the last drop of information out of the child.

'Come on, tell us,' urged one of the women for perhaps the hundredth time. 'How did you see them?'

'Let my two eyes drop out right here if I'm lying,' the child repeated again and again with unabated excitement. 'The Agha's son came in, and then they lay down, both of them, and did things . . . I was watching through a chink in the wall. Uncle Osman's wife, you know, was crying. I can't do it, she was saying, and she was sobbing away all the time. Then the Agha's son pulled off those shiny yellow boots of his . . . Then I ran right here to tell Mother.'

The news spread through the village like wildfire. People could talk about nothing else. Seedy Doneh, for one, seemed to have made it her job to leave no man or woman uninformed. As she scoured the village for new listeners, she chanced upon Osman himself.

'Haven't you heard what's come upon you?' she said, drawing him aside behind the wall of a hut. 'You're disgraced, you jackass. The Agha's son has got his fingers up your wife's skirt. Try and clear your good name now if you can!'

Osman did not seem to understand.

'I don't know . . .' he murmured, shrugging his shoulders. 'I'll have to ask the Mistress. What would the Agha's son want with my wife?'

Doneh was incensed.

'What would he want with her, blockhead?' she screamed. 'Damn you, your wife's become a whore, that's what! She's turned your home into a brothel. Anyone can come in and have her.' She flounced off still screaming. 'I spit on you! I spit on your manhood . . .'

Osman was upset.

'What are you shouting for, woman?' he called after her. 'People will think something's wrong. I have to ask the Mistress. She knows everything. How should I know?'

He started walking home, his long arms dangling at his sides as though they had been hitched to his shoulders as an afterthought, his fingers sticking out wide apart as was his habit. This time he was waylaid by their next-door neighbour, Zeynep, who planted herself before him and tackled him at the top of her voice.

'Ah Osman! You'd be better off dead! Why don't you go and bury yourself? The whole village knows about it. Your wife . . . The Agha's son . . . Ah Osman, how could you have brought such a woman into your home? Where's your honour now? Disgraced . . . Ah Osman!'

He stared at her in bewilderment.

'How should I know?' he stammered, his huge hands opening out like pitchforks. 'The Mistress knows all about such things. I'll go and ask her.'

Zeynep turned her back on him in exasperation, her large skirt ballooning about her legs.

'Go bury yourself, Osman! I hope I see you dead after this.'

A group of children were playing tipcat near by. Suddenly one of them broke into a chant.

'Go bury yourself, Osman . . . See you dead, Osman . . .'

The other children joined in mechanically without inter-rupting their game.

Osman stared at them and turned away.

'How should I know?' he muttered. 'I must go to the Mistress.'

He found Huru sitting at her spinning-wheel. Fadik was there too, squatting near the hearth and listlessly chewing mastic-gum.

'Mistress,' said Osman, 'have you heard what Seedy Doneh's saying? She's saying I'm disgraced . . .'

Huru stepped on the pedal forcefully and brought the wheel to a stop.

'What's that?' she said. 'What about Seedy Doneh?'

'I don't know . . . She said Fadik . . .'

'Look here,' said Huru, 'you mustn't believe those lying

bitches. You've got a good wife. Where would you find such a woman?'

'I don't know. Go bury yourself, they said. The children too . . .'

'Shut up,' cried Huru, annoyed. 'People always gossip about a beautiful woman. They go looking for the mote in their neighbour's eye without seeing the beam in their own. They'd better hold their peace because I've got a tongue in my head too . . .'

Osman smiled with relief.

'How could I know?' he said.

Down in the villages of the Chukurova plain, a sure sign of oncoming spring is when the women are seen with their heads on one another's lap, picking the lice out of one another's hair. So it was, on one of the first warm days of the year. A balmy sun shone caressingly down on the fields and village, and not a leaf stirred. A group of women were sitting before their huts on the dusty ground, busy with the lice and wagging their tongues for all they were worth. An acrid odour of sweat hung about the group. Seedy Doneh was rummaging in the hair of a large woman who was stretched full length on the ground. She decided that she had been silent long enough.

'No,' she declared suddenly, 'it's not as you say, sister! He didn't force her or any such thing. She simply fell for him the minute she saw those shiny yellow boots. If you're going to believe Huru! . . . She's got to deny it, of course.'

'That Huru was born with a silver spoon in her mouth,' said white-haired, toothless old Zala, wiping her blood-stained fingers on her ragged skirt. 'Hollow Osman's been slaving for her like twenty men ever since she took him in, a kid the size of your hand! And all for a mere pittance of food. And now there's the woman too. Tell me, what's there left for Huru to do?'

'Ah,' sighed another woman, 'fortune has smiled on Huru, she has indeed! She's got two people serving her now.'

'And both for nothing,' old Zala reminded her.

'What it amounts to,' said Seedy Doneh spitefully, 'is that Huru used to have one wife and now she's got two. Osman was always a woman, and as for Fadik she's a real woman. He-he!'

'That she is, a real woman!' the others agreed.

'Huru says the Agha's son took her by force,' pursued Doneh. 'All right, but what about the others? What about those lining up at her door all through the night, eh? She never says no to any one of them, does she? She takes in everyone, young and old.'

'The Lady Bountiful, that's what she is,' said Elif. 'And do you know something? Now that Fadik's here, the young men are leaving Omarja's yellow bitch in peace . . .'

'They've got somewhere better to go!' cackled the others.

Omarja's dumpy wife jumped up from where she was sitting on the edge of the group.

'Now look here, Elif!' she cried. 'What's all this about our yellow dog? Stop blackening people's characters, will you?'

'Well, it's no lie, is it?' Doneh challenged her. 'When was that bitch ever at your door where she should be all night? No, instead, there she came trotting up a-mornings with a rope dangling from her neck!'

'Don't go slandering our dog,' protested Omarja's wife. 'Why, if Omarja hears this, he'll kill the poor creature. Upon my word he will!'

'Go on!' said Doneh derisively. 'Don't you come telling me that Omarja doesn't know his yellow bitch is the paramour of all the village youths! What about that time when Stumpy Veli caught some of them down by the river, all taking it in turns over her? Is there anyone in this village who didn't hear of that? It's no use trying to whitewash your bitch to us!'

Omarja's wife was alarmed.

'Don't, sister,' she pleaded. 'Omarja'll shoot the dog, that's sure . . .'

'Well, I'm not to blame for that, sister,' retorted Doneh tartly. 'Anyway, the bitch'll be all right now that Fadik's around. And so will Kurdish Velo's donkey . . .'

Kurdish Velo's wife began to fidget nervously.

'Not our fault,' she blurted out in her broken Turkish. 'We lock our donkey in, but they come and break the door! Velo furious. Velo say people round here savage. He say, with an animal deadly sin! He say he kill someone. Then he complain to the Headman. Velo going sell this donkey.'

'You know what I think?' interposed Seedy Doneh. 'They're going to make it hot for her in this village. Yes, they'll do what they did to Esheh.'

'Poor Esheh,' sighed old Zala. 'What a woman she was before her man got thrown into prison! She would never have come to that, but she had no one to protect her. May they rot in hell, those that forced her into it! But she is dead and gone, poor thing.'

'Eh!' said Doneh. 'How could she be otherwise after the youths of five villages had done with her?' She straightened up. 'Look here, sister,' she said to the woman whose head was on her lap, 'I couldn't get through your lice in days! They say the Government's invented some medicine for lice which they call Dee-Dee. Ah, if only we had a spoonful of that . . . Do you know, women, that Huru keeps watch over Fadik at night? She tells the youths when to come in and then drives them out with a stick. Ha-ha, and she wants us to believe in Fadik's virtue . . .'

'That's because it suits her. Where will she find people who'll work for nothing like those two?'

'Well, the lads are well provided for this year,' snickered Doneh. 'Who knows but that Huru may hop in and help Fadik out!'

Just then, Huru loomed up from behind a hut. She was a large woman with a sharp chin and a wrinkled face. Her greying hair was always carefully dyed with henna.

'Whores!' she shouted at the top of her voice, as she bore down upon them with arms akimbo. 'City trollops! You get hold of a poor fellow's wife and let your tongues go wagging away. Tell me, are you any better than she? What do you want of this harmless mountain girl?' She pounced on Doneh who cringed back. 'As for you, you filthy shitty-assed bitch, you'll shut your mouth or I'll start telling the truth about you and that husband of yours who pretends he's a man. You know me, don't you?'

Doneh blenched.

'Me, sister?' she stammered. 'Me? I never . . . Other people's good name . . .'

The women were dispersing hastily. Only Kurdish Velo's wife, unaware of what was going on, continued picking lice out of her companion's hair.

'Velo says in our country women like this burnt alive. He says there no virtue in this Chukurova. No honour . . .'

The eastern sky had only just begun to pale as, with a great hullabaloo and calls and cries, the women and children drove the cattle out to pasture. Before their houses, red-aproned matrons were busy at the churns beating yoghurt. The damp air smelled of spring.

Osman had long ago yoked the oxen and was waiting at Huru's door.

She appeared in the doorway.

'Osman, my lion,' she said, 'you're not to come back until you've ploughed through the whole field. The girl Aysheh will look after your food and get you some bedding. Mind you do the sowing properly, my child. Husneh's hard pressed this year. And there's your wife to feed too now . . .'

Husneh was Huru's only child, whom in a moment of aberration she had given in marriage to Ali Efendi, a low-salaried tax-collector. All the product of her land, everything Huru had, was for this daughter.

Osman did not move or say a word. He stood there in the half light, a large black shadow near the yoked oxen whose tails were flapping their legs in slow rhythm.

Huru stepped up to him.

'What's the matter with you, Osman, my child,' she said anxiously. 'Is anything wrong?'

'Mistress,' whispered Osman, 'it's what Seedy Doneh's saying. And Zeynep too . . . That my house . . . I don't know . . .'

Huru flared up.

'Shut up, you spineless dolt,' she cried. 'Don't you come babbling to me about the filthy inventions of those city trollops. I paid that broken-nosed thief a hundred good banknotes for the girl, didn't I? Did I ask you for as much as a lira? You listen to me. You can find fault with pure gold, but not with Fadik. Don't let me hear such nonsense from you again!'

Osman hesitated.

'I don't know . . .' he murmured, as he turned at last and drove the oxen off before him.

It was mid-morning. A bright sun glowed over the sparkling fields.

Osman was struggling with the lean, emaciated oxen, which after ploughing through only one acre had stretched themselves on the ground and simply refused to budge. Flushed and breathless, he let himself drop on to a mound and took his head in his hands. After a while, he rose and tried pulling the animals up by the tail.

'Accursed beasts,' he muttered. 'The Mistress says Husneh's in need this year. Get up this minute, accursed beasts!'

He pushed and heaved, but to no avail. Suddenly in a burst of fury, he flung himself on the black ox, dug his teeth into its nose and shook it with all his might. Then he straightened up and looked about him sheepishly.

'If anyone saw me . . .' He swore as he spat out blood. 'What can I do? Husneh's in need and there's Fadik to feed too. And now these heathen beasts . . . I don't know.'

It was in this state of perplexity that Stumpy Veli found him when he strolled over from a neighbouring field.

'So the team's collapsed, eh?' he commented. 'Well, it was to be expected. Look at how their ribs are sticking out. You won't be able to get anything out of them.'

'I don't know,' muttered Osman faintly. 'Husneh's in a bad way and I got married . . .'

'And a fine mess that's landed you in,' burst out Veli angrily. 'You'd have been better off dead!'

'I don't know,' said Osman. 'The Mistress paid a hundred liras for her . . .'

Stumpy Veli took hold of his arm and made him sit down.

'Look, Osman,' he said, 'the villagers told me to talk to you. They say you're giving the village a bad name. Ever since the Agha's son took up with your wife, all the other youths have followed suit and your house is just like a brothel now. The villagers say you've got to repudiate her. If you don't, they'll drive you both out. The honour of the whole village is at stake, and you know honour doesn't grow on trees . . .'

Osman, his head hanging down, was as still as a statue. A stray ant had caught his eye.

What's this ant doing around here at this time of the day, he wondered to himself. Where can its nest be?

Veli nudged him sharply.

'Damn you, man!' he cried. 'Think what'll happen if the police get wind of this. She hasn't got any papers. Why, if the gendarmes once lay their hands on her, you know how it'll be. They'll play around with her for months, poor creature.'

Osman started as though an electric current had been sent through his large frame.

'I haven't got any papers either,' he whispered.

Veli drew nearer. Their shoulders touched. Osman's were trembling fiftully.

'Papers are the business of the Government,' Veli said. 'You and me, we can't understand such things. If we did, then what would we need a Government for? Now, listen to me. If the gendarmes get hold of her, we'll be the laughing-stock of villages for miles around. We'll never be able to hold up our heads again in the Chukurova. You mustn't trifle with the honour of the whole village. Get rid of her before she drags you into more trouble.'

'But where will I be without her?' protested Osman. 'I'll die, that's all. Who'll do my washing? Who'll cook bulgur pilaff for me? I'll starve to death if I have to eat gruel again every day. I just can't do without her.'

'The villagers will buy you another woman,' said Veli. 'We'll collect the money among us. A better woman, an honourable one, and beautiful too ... I'll go up into the mountain villages and pick one for you myself. Just you pack this one off quickly ...'

'I don't know,' said Osman. 'It's the Mistress knows about these things.'

Veli was exasperated.

'Damn the Mistress!' he shouted. 'It's up to you, you idiot!'

Then he softened. He tried persuasion again. He talked and talked. He talked himself hoarse, but Osman sat there immovable as a rock, his mouth clamped tight. Finally Veli spat in his face and stalked off.

It was well on in the afternoon when it occurred to Osman to unyoke the team. He had not stirred since Veli's departure. As for the oxen, they had just lain there placidly chewing the cud. He managed to get them to their feet and let them wander about the field, while he walked back to the village. He made straight for the Agha's house and waited in the yard, not speaking to anyone, until he saw the Agha's son riding in, the bridle of his horse lathered with sweat.

The Agha's son was taken aback. He dismounted quickly, but Osman waylaid him.

'Listen,' he pleaded, 'you're the son of our all-powerful Agha. What do you want with my wife?'

The Agha's son became the colour of his famous boots. He hastily pulled a five-lira note out of his pocket and thrust it into Osman's hand.

'Take this,' he mumbled and hurried away.

'But you're a great big Agha's son!' cried Osman after him.
'Why do you want to drive her away? What harm has she
done you? You're a great big . . .'

He was crushed. He stumbled away towards Huru's house,
the five-lira note still in his hand.

At the sight of Osman, Huru blew her top.

'What are you doing here, you feeble-minded ass?' she
shouted. 'Didn't I tell you not to come back until you'd
finished all the ploughing? Do you want to ruin me, you
idiot?'

'Wait, Mistress,' stammered Osman. 'Listen . . .'

'Listen, he says! Damn the fool!'

'Mistress,' he pleaded, 'let me explain . . .'

Huru glared at him.

'Mistress, you haven't heard. You don't know what the
villagers are going to do to me. They're going to throw me
out of this village. Stumpy Veli said so. He said the police
. . . He said papers . . . We haven't got any papers. Fadik
hasn't and I haven't either. He said the gendarmes would
carry Fadik away and do things to her. He said I must
repudiate her because my house is a brothel. That's what he
said. I said the Mistress knows these things . . . She paid
the hundred liras . . .'

Huru was dancing with fury. She rushed out into
the village square and began howling at the top of her
voice.

'Bastards! So she's a thorn in your flesh, this poor fellow's
wife! If you want to drive whores out of this village why
don't you start with your own wives and daughters? You'd
better look for whores in your own homes, pimps that you
are, all of you! And tell your sons to leave poor folks'
women alone . . .'

Then she turned to Osman and gave him a push.

'Off you go! To the fields! No one's going to do anything to your wife. Not while I'm alive.'

The villagers had gathered in the square and had heard Huru out in profound silence. As soon as she was gone, though, they started muttering among themselves.

'Who does that bitch think she is, abusing the whole village like that? . . .'

The Agha, Wolf Mahmut, had heard her too.

'You just wait, Huru,' he said grinding his teeth. 'If you think you're going to get away with this . . .'

The night was dark, a thick damp darkness that seemed to cling to the face and hands. Huru had been waiting for some time now, concealed in the blackest shadow of the barn, when suddenly she perceived a stirring in the darkness, and a voice was calling softly at the door.

'Fadik! Open up, girl. It's me . . .'

The door creaked open and a shadow glided in. An uncontrollable trembling seized Huru. She gripped her stick and flung herself on the door. It was unbolted and went crashing back against the wall. As she stood there trying to pierce the darkness, a few vague figures hustled by and made their escape. Taken by surprise, she hurled out a vitriolic oath and started groping about until she discovered Fadik crouching in a corner. She seized her by the hair and began to beat her with the stick.

'Bitch!' she hissed. 'To think I was standing up for you . . .'

Fadik did not utter a sound as the blows rained down on her. At last Huru, exhausted, let go of her.

'Get up,' she ordered, 'and light some kindling.'

Fadik raked out the dying embers and with much puffing and blowing managed to light a stick of torchwood. A pale honeyed light fell dimly over the stacked hay. There was an old pallet in one corner and a few kitchen utensils, but nothing else to show that the place was lived in.

Huru took Fadik's hand and looked at her sternly.

'Didn't you promise me, girl, that you'd never do it again?'

Fadik's head hung low.

'Do you know, you bitch,' continued Huru, 'what the villagers are going to do? They're going to kick you out of the village. Do you hear me?'

Fadik stirred a little. 'Mistress, I swear I didn't go after them! They just came in spite of everything.'

'Listen to me, girl,' said Huru. 'Do you know what happened to Esheh? That's what you'll come to if you're not careful. They're like ravening wolves, these men. If you fall into their clutches, they'll tear you to shreds. To shreds, I tell you!'

'But Mistress, I swear I never did anything to—'

'You must bolt your door because they'll be after you whether you do anything or not, and their pimps of fathers will put the blame on me. It's my hundred liras they can't swallow. They're dying to see it go to pot . . . Just like Esheh you'll be. They had no one in the world, she and her man, and when Ali was thrown into jail she was left all alone. He'd lifted a sheep from the Agha's flock and bought clothes and shoes for their son. A lovely child he was, three years old . . . Ali doted on him. But there he was in jail, and that yellow-booted good-for-nothing was soon after Esheh like the plague. She kept him at arm's length for as long as she could, poor Esheh, but he got what he wanted in the end. Then he turned her over to those ravening wolves. . . They dragged her about from village to village, from mountain to mountain. Twenty, thirty good-for-nothings . . . Her child was left among strangers, the little boy she had loved so. He died . . . Those who saw her said she was like a consumptive, thin and grey, but still they wouldn't let her go, those scoundrels. Then one day the village dogs came in all smeared with blood, and an eagle was circling over the plain. So the men went to look, and they found Esheh, her body half devoured by the dogs . . . They'd made her dance naked for them . . . They'd done all sorts of things to her. Yes, they as good as killed her. That's what the police said when they came up from the town. And when Ali heard of it, he died of grief in jail. Yes, my girl, you've got Esheh's fate before you. It isn't my hundred liras that I care for, it's you. As for Osman, I can always find another woman for him. Now I've warned you. Just call me if they come again. Esheh was all alone in the world. You've got me, at least. Do you swear to do as I'm telling you?'

'I swear it, Mistress,' said Fadik.

Huru was suddenly very tired.

'Well, I'm going. You'll call me, won't you?'

As soon as she was gone, the youths crept out of the darkness and sneaked into the barn again.

'Hey, Fadik,' they whispered. 'Huru was lying to you, girl. Esheh just killed herself . . .'

There was a stretch of grass in front of the Agha's house, and on one side of it dung had been heaped to the size of a small hillock. The dung steamed in the early morning sun and not a breath stirred the warm air. A cock climbed to the top of the heap. It scraped the dung, stretched its neck and crowed triumphantly, flapping its wings.

The group of villagers squatting about on the grass silently

eyed the angry Agha. Wolf Mahmut was a huge man whose
shadow when he was sitting was as large as that of an average
man standing up. He was never seen without a frayed,
checked overcoat, the only one in the village, that he had
been wearing for years now.

He was toying irritably with his metal-framed glasses when
Stumpy Veli, who had been sent for a while ago, made his
appearance. The Agha glared at him.

'Is this the way you get things done, you fraud?' he
expostulated. 'So you'd have Hollow Osman eating out of
your hand in no time, eh?'

Stumpy Veli seemed to shrink to half his size.

'Agha,' he said, 'I tried everything. I talked and talked. I
told him the villagers would drive them both out. I warned
him of the gendarmes. All right, he said, I'll send her away.
And then he didn't . . . If you ask me, Huru's at the bottom
of it all.'

The others stirred. 'That she is!' they agreed.

Mahmut Agha jumped up. 'I'll get even with her,' he
growled.

'That, you will, Agha,' they assented. 'But . . .'

'We've put up with that old whore long enough,' continued
the Agha, sitting down again.

'Yes, Agha,' said Stumpy Veli, 'but, you see, she relies on
her son-in-law Ali, the tax-collector. They'd better stop
treading on my toes, she said, or I'll have Ali strip this village
bare . . .'

'He can't do anything,' said the Agha. 'I don't owe the
Government a bean.'

'But we do, Agha,' interposed one of the men. 'He can
come here and take away our blankets and rugs, whatever
we have . . .'

'It's because of Huru that he hasn't fleeced this village up to now,' said another. 'We owe a lot of money, Agha.'

'Well, what are we to do then?' cried Mahmut Agha angrily. 'All our youths have left the plough and the fields and are after the woman night and day like rutting bulls. At this rate, the whole village'll starve this year.'

An old man spoke up in a tremulous voice. 'I'm dead for one,' he wailed. 'That woman's ruined my hearth. High morning it is already. Go to the plough, my son, I beg the boy. We'll starve if you don't plough. But he won't listen. He's always after that woman. I've lost my son because of that whore. I'm too old to plough any more. I'll starve this year. I'll go and throw myself at Huru's feet. There's nothing else to do . . .'

The Agha rose abruptly. 'That Huru!' He gritted his teeth. 'I'll settle her account.'

He strode away.

The villagers looked up hopefully. 'Mahmut Agha'll settle her account,' they muttered. 'He'll find a way . . .'

The Agha heard them and swelled with pride. 'Yes, Mahmut Agha'll settle her account,' he repeated grimly to himself.

He stopped before a hut and called out.

'Hatije Woman! Hatije!'

A middle-aged woman rushed out wiping her hands on her apron.

'Mahmut Agha!' she cried. 'Welcome to our home. You never visit us these days.' Then she whirled back. 'Get up, you damned lazybones,' she shouted angrily. 'It's high morning, and look who's here.'

Mahmut Agha followed her inside.

'Look, Agha,' she complained, pointing to her son, 'it's high morning and Halil still abed!'

Startled at the sight of the Agha, Halil sprang up and drew on his black shalvar-trousers shamefacedly, while his mother continued with her lamentations.

'Ah, Mahmut Agha, you don't know what's befallen us! You don't know, may I kiss your feet, my Agha, or you wouldn't have us on your land any longer . . . Ah, Mahmut Agha! This accursed son of mine . . . I would have seen him dead and buried, yes, buried in this black earth before . . .'

'What are you cursing the lad for?' Mahmut Agha interrupted her. 'Wait, just tell me first.'

'Ah, Agha, if you knew! It was full day when he came home this night. And it's the same every night, the same ever since Hollow Osman's woman came to the village. He lies abed all through the livelong day. Who'll do the ploughing, I ask you? We'll starve this year. Ah, Mahmut Agha, do something! Please do something . . .'

'You go outside a little, will you, Hatije,' said the Agha. Then he turned to Halil, stretching out his long, wrinkled neck which had become as red as a turkey's. 'Listen to me, my boy, this has got to end. You must get this whore out of our village and give her to the youths of another village, any village. She's got to go and you'll do it. It's an order. Do you hear me?'

'Why, Agha!' Halil said ingratiatingly. 'Is that what's worrying you? I'll get hold of her this very night and turn her over to Jelil from Ortakli village. You can count on me.'

The Agha's spirits rose.

'Hatije,' he called out, 'come in here. See how I'm getting you out of this mess? And all the village too . . . Let that Huru know who she's dealing with in the future. They call me

Wolf Mahmut and I know how to put her nose out of joint.'

Long before dawn, piercing shrieks startled the echoes in the village.

'Bastards! Pimps!' Huru was howling. 'You won't get away with this, not on your life you won't. My hundred liras were too much for you to swallow, eh, you fiends? You were jealous of this poor fellow's wife, eh? But you just wait and see, Wolf Mahmut! I'll set the tax-collector after you all in no time. I'll get even with you if I have to spend my last penny! I'll bribe the Mudir, the Kaymakam, all the officials. I'll send telegrams to Ankara, to Ismet Pasha, to the head of the Democrats. I'll have you all dragged into court, rotting away in police-stations. I'll get my own back on you for Fadik's sake.'

She paused to get her breath and was off again even louder than before.

Fadik had disappeared, that was the long and the short of it. Huru soon found out that someone else was missing too, Huseyin's half-witted son, The Tick.

'Impossible,' she said. 'The Tick ravishing women? Not to save his life, he couldn't! This is just another trick of those good-for-nothings . . .'

'But really, Huru,' the villagers tried to persuade her, 'he was after her all the time. Don't you know he gathered white snails in the hills, threaded them into a necklace and offered it to Fadik, and she hung it up on her wall as a keep-sake? That's the plain truth, Huru.'

'I don't believe it,' Huru said stubbornly. 'I wouldn't even if I saw them together with my own eyes . . .'

The next day it started raining, that sheer, plumbline torrent

which sets in over the Chukurova for days. The minute the
bad news had reached him, Osman had abandoned his
plough and had rushed back to the village. He was standing
now motionless at Huru's door, the peak of his cap drooping
over his eyes. His wet clothes clung to his flesh, glistening
darkly, and his rawhide boots were clogged with mud.

'Come in out of the rain, Osman, do!' Huru kept urging
him.

'I can't. I don't know . . .' was all he could say.

'Now, look here, Osman,' said Huru. 'She's gone, so
what? Let them have that bitch. I'll find you a good woman,
my Osman. Never mind the money. I'll spend twice as much
on a new wife for you. Just you come in out of the rain.'

Osman never moved.

'Listen, Osman. I've sent word to Ali. Come and levy the
taxes at once, I said. Have no mercy on these ungrateful
wretches. If you don't fleece them to their last rag, I said,
you needn't count on me as a mother again. You'll see what
I'm going to do to them, my Osman. You just come inside . . .'

The rain poured down straight and thick as the warp in a
loom, and Osman still stood there, his chin resting on his
staff, like a thick tree whose branches have been lopped
off.

Huru appealed to the neighbours. Two men came and
pulled and pushed, but he seemed nailed to the ground.
It was well in the afternoon when he stirred and began to
pace the village from one end to the other, his head sunk
between his shoulders and the rain streaming down his body.

'Poor fellow, he's gone mad,' opined the villagers.

A few strong men finally carried him home. They un-
dressed him and put him to bed.

Huru sat down beside him. 'Look, Osman, I'll get you a

new woman even if it costs me a thousand liras. You mustn't distress yourself so. Just for a woman . . .'

The next morning he was more his normal self, but no amount of reasoning or pleading from Huru could induce him to go back to the field. He left the house and resumed his pacing up and down.

The villagers had really begun to feel sorry for him now.

'Alas, poor Osman!' they murmured as he passed between the huts.

Osman heard them and heaved deep, heart-rending sighs. And still he roamed aimlessly round and round.

Wolf Mahmut should have known better. Why, the whole village saw with half an eye what a rascal Halil was! How could he be trusted to give up a woman once he had got her into his hands? He had indeed got Fadik out of the way, but what he had done was to shut her up in one of the empty sheep-pens in the hills beyond the village, and there he had posted The Tick to guard her.

'Play around with her if you like,' he had told him contemptuously. 'But if you let her give you the slip—' and he had seized The Tick's wrist and squeezed it until it hurt— 'you're as good as dead.'

Though twenty years old, The Tick was so scraggy and undersized that at first glance people would take him to be only ten. His arms and legs were as thin as matchsticks and he walked sideways like a crab. He had always had a way of clinging tenaciously to people or objects he took a fancy to, which even as a child had earned him his nickname. No one had ever called him by his real name and it looked as though his own mother had forgotten it too . . .

Halil would come every evening bringing food for Fadik and The Tick, and he would leave again just before dawn.

But it was not three days before the village youths found out what was going on. After that there was a long queue every night outside the sheep-pen. They would take it in turns, heedless of Fadik's tears and howls, and at daybreak, singing and firing their guns as though in a wedding procession, they would make their way back to the village.

Night was falling and Fadik began to tremble like a leaf. They would not be long now. They would come again and torture her. She was weak with fear and exhaustion. For the past two days, her gorge had risen at the very sight of food, and she lay there on the dirt floor, hardly able to move, her whole body covered with bruises and wounds.

The Tick was dozing away near the door of the pen.

Fadik tried to plead with him. 'Let me go, brother,' she begged. 'I'll die if I have to bear another night of this.'

The Tick half-opened his eyes. 'I can't,' he replied.

'But if I die, it'll be your fault. Before God it will . . . Please let me go.'

'Why should it be my fault?' said The Tick. 'I didn't bring you here, did I?'

'They'll never know. You'll say you fell asleep. I'll go off and hide somewhere. I'll go back to my mother . . .'

'I can't,' said The Tick. 'Halil would kill me if I let you go.'

'But I want to go to my mother,' she cried desperately. 'You must let me go. Please let me go . . .'

It was dark now and the sound of singing drifted up from the village.

Fadik was seized with a violent fit of trembling. 'They're coming,' she said. 'Let me get away now, brother. Save me! If you save me, I'll be your woman. I'll do anything . . .'

But The Tick had not been nicknamed for nothing.

'They'd kill me,' he said. 'Why should I die because of you? And Halil's promised to buy me a pair of shoes, too. I'm not going to go without shoes because of you.'

Fadik broke into wild sobbing. There was no hope now.

'Oh, God,' she wept, 'what shall I do now? Oh, Mother, why was I ever born?'

They lined up as usual at the entrance to the pen. The first one went in and a nerve-racking scream rose from Fadik, a scream that would have moved the most hardened of hearts. But the youths were deaf to everything. In they went, one after the other, and soon Fadik's screams died down. Not even a moan came out of her.

There were traces of blood on the ground at the back of the sheep-pen. Halil and the Agha's son had had a fight the night before and the Agha's son had split open Halil's head.

'The woman's mine,' Halil had insisted. 'I've a right to go in first.'

'No, you haven't,' the Agha's son had contended. 'I'm going to be the first.'

The other youths had taken sides and joined the fray which had lasted most of the night, and it was a bedraggled band that wended back to the village that night.

Bowed down with grief, Hatije Woman came weeping to the Muhtar.

'My son is dying,' she cried. 'He's at his last gasp, my poor Halil, and it's the Agha's son who did it, all because of that whore of Huru's. Ah, Muhtar, if my son dies what's to become of me? There he lies struggling for life, the only hope of my hearth. But I won't let the Agha get away with this. I'll go to the Government. An old woman's only prop, I'll say . . .'

The Muhtar had great difficulty in talking Hatije out of her purpose.

'You go back home, Hatije Woman,' he said when she had calmed down a little, 'and don't worry. I'll deal with this business.'

He summoned the Agha and the elders, and a long discussion ensued. It would not do to hand over the woman to the police-station. These rapacious gendarmes! . . . The honour of the whole village was at stake. And if they passed her on to the youths of another village, Huru was sure to find out and bring her back. She would not rest until she did.

After long deliberation, they came to a decision at last. The woman would be returned to Osman, but on one condition. He would take himself off with her to some distant place and never appear in the village again. They had no doubt that Osman, grateful to have Fadik back to himself, would accept. And that would cook Huru's goose too. She would lose both the woman and Osman. It would teach her to insult a whole village!

A couple of men went to find Osman and brought him back with them to the Muhtar's house.

'Sit down,' they urged him, but he just stood there grasping his staff, staring about him with bloodshot eyes. His clothes hung down torn and crumpled and stained yellow from his lying all wet on the hay. His hair was a tangled, clotted mass and bits of straw clung to the stubble on his chin.

Wolf Mahmut took off his glasses and fidgeted with them.

'Osman, my lad,' he remonstrated, 'what's this state you're in? And all for a woman! Does a man let himself break down like this just for a woman? You'll die if you go on like this . . .'

'I don't know,' said Osman. 'I'll die . . .'

'See here, Osman,' said the Agha. 'We're here to help you. We'll get your woman back for you from out of those rascals' hands. Then you'll take her and go. You'll both get away from here, as far as possible. But you're not to tell Huru. She mustn't know where you are.'

'You see, Osman,' said Stumpy Veli, 'how good the Agha's being to you. Your own father wouldn't have done more.'

'But you're not to tell Huru,' the Agha insisted. 'If you do, she'll never let you go away. And then the youths will come and take your woman away from you again. And how will you ever get yourself another woman?'

'And who'll wash your clothes then?' added Stumpy Veli. 'Who'll cook your bulgur pilaff for you? You mustn't breathe a word to Huru. Just take Fadik and go off to the villages around Antep. Once there, you'll be sure to get a job on a farm. You'll be much better off than you ever were with Huru, and you'll have your woman with you too . . .'

'But how can I do that?' protested Osman. 'The Mistress paid a hundred liras for Fadik.'

'We'll collect that much among us,' the Agha assured him. 'Don't you worry about that. We'll see that Huru gets her money back. You just take the woman and go.'

'I don't know,' said Osman. His eyes filled with tears and he swallowed. 'The Mistress has always been so good to me . . . How can I . . . Just for a woman . . .'

'If you tell Huru, you're lost,' said the Agha. 'Is Huru the only mistress in the world? Aren't there other villages in this country? Take the woman and go. You'll never find another woman like Fadik. Listen, Veli'll tell you where she is and tomorrow you'll take her and go.'

Osman bowed his head. He thought for a long time. Then he looked up at them.

'I won't tell her,' he said at last. 'Why should I want to stay here? There are other villages . . .'

Before dawn the next day, he set out for the sheep-pen which Stumpy Veli had indicated.

'I don't know . . .' he hesitated at the door. 'I don't know . . .' Then he called out softly. 'Fadik? Fadik, girl . . .'

There was no answer. Trembling with hope and fear, he stepped in, then stopped aghast. Fadik was lying there on the dirt floor with only a few tatters left to cover her naked body. Her huge eyes were fixed vacantly on the branches that roofed the pen.

He stood frozen, his eyes filling with tears. Then he bent his large body over her.

'Fadik,' he whispered, 'are you all right?'

Her answering moan shook him to the core. He slipped off his shirt and helped her into it. Then he noticed The Tick who had shrunk back into a corner, trying to make himself invisible. Osman moved on him threateningly.

'Uncle Osman,' cried The Tick shaking with fear, 'I didn't do it. It was Halil. He said he'd buy me a pair of shoes . . . And Fadik would have died if I hadn't been here . . .'

Osman turned away, heaved Fadik on to his back swiftly and threw himself out of the pen.

The mountain peaks were pale and the sun was about to rise. A few white clouds floated in the sky and a cool breeze caressed his face. The earth was wet with dew.

The Tick was scurrying off towards the village.

'Brother,' Osman called after him, 'go to the Mistress and tell her I thank her for all she's done for me, but I have to go. Tell her to forgive me . . .'

He set out in the opposite direction with Fadik on his back. He walked without a break until the sun was up the height of two minarets. Then he lowered Fadik to the ground and sat down opposite her. They looked at each other for a long while without speaking.

'Tell me,' said Osman. 'Where shall we go now? I don't know . . .'

Fadik moaned.

The air smelled of spring and the earth steamed under the sun.

The White Trousers

It was hot. The boy Mustafa held the shoe listlessly and gazed out of the shop at the sun-impacted street with its uneven cobbles. He felt he would never be able to mend this shoe. It was the most tattered thing he had ever come across. He looked up tentatively, but the cobbler was bent over his work. He placed the shoe on the bench and hammered in a nail haphazardly.

'I can't do it,' he murmured at last.

'What's that, Mustafa?' said the cobbler, raising his head for a moment. 'Why, you haven't begun to try yet!'

'But, Master,' protested the boy, 'it comes apart as soon as I put in a stitch . . .'

The cobbler was silent.

Mustafa tackled the shoe again. His face was running with sweat and the sun had dropped nearer the distant hills when Hassan Bey, a well-to-do friend of the cobbler's, stepped into the shop.

'My friend,' he said, 'I need a boy to help fire my brick-kiln. Will you let me have this one? Only for three days.'

'Would you work at the brick-kiln, Mustafa?' asked the cobbler. 'It's for three days and three nights too, you know . . .'

'The pay is one and a half liras a day,' said Hassan Bey. 'All you'll have to do is give a hand to Jumali. You know Jumali who lives down by the river? He's a good man, won't let you work yourself out.'

Mustafa's black eyes shone.

36

'All right, Uncle Hassan,' he said. 'But I'll have to ask Mother . . .'

'Well, ask her, and be at my orange grove tomorrow. The kiln's in the field next to it. You'll start work in the afternoon. I won't be there, but you'll find Jumali.'

The cobbler paid him twenty-five kurush a week. A whole month and only one lira! It was July already, and a pair of summer shoes cost two liras, a pair of white trousers three . . . But now, four and a half liras would be his for only three days' work! What a stroke of luck! . . . First you wash your hands, but properly, with soap . . . Then you unwrap the white canvas shoes . . . Your socks must be white too. You must be careful, very careful with the white trousers. They get soiled so quickly. Your fingers should hardly touch them. And so to the bridge where the girls stroll in the cool of the evening, the breeze swelling their skirts . . . The breeze tautening the white trousers against your legs . . .

'Mother!' he cried, bursting into the house. 'I'm going to fire Hassan Bey's brick-kiln with Jumali!'

'Who says so? Certainly not!'

'But, Mother . . .'

'My child, you don't know what firing a kiln means. Can you go without sleep for three days and three nights? God knows I have trouble enough waking you up in the morning!'

'But, Mother, this is different . . .'

'You'll fall asleep, I tell you. You'll never stand it.'

'Look, Mother, you know Sami, Tewfik Bey's son Sami?' he said hopefully.

'Well?'

'Those white trousers of his and the white shoes? Snow-white! I've got a silk shirt in the trunk. I'll wear that too. Wouldn't I look well?'

Mustafa knew his mother. The tears rose to her eyes. She bowed her head.

'Wouldn't I, Mother? Now, wouldn't I?'

'My darling, you'd look well in anything . . .'

'Vayis the tailor'll do it for me. Mother dear, say I can go!'

'Well, I don't know . . .' she said doubtfully.

He saw she was giving in and flung himself on her neck.

'When I'm big . . .' he began.

'You'll work very hard.'

'And then?' he prompted.

'You'll make a beautiful orange grove of that empty field of ours near the stream. You'll have a horse of your own to ride . . . You'll order navy blue suits from tailors in Adana . . .'

'And then?'

'Then you'll tile the roof of our house so it won't let in the rain.'

'Then?'

'You'll be just like your father.'

'And if my father hadn't died?'

'You'd have gone to school and studied and become a great man . . .'

'But now?'

'If your Father had been alive . . .'

'Look,' said Mustafa, 'I'll have a gold watch when I'm big, won't I?'

The next morning he was up and away before sunrise. The dust on the road felt cool and soft under his bare feet. A flood of light was surging up behind the hill. When he came to the kiln, the sun was sitting on the crest like a great round ember. He bent over to the mouth of the kiln. It was dark inside. Around it brushwood had been heaped in little hillocks.

It was almost noon when Jumali arrived. He was a big man who walked ponderously, picking his way. Ignoring Mustafa, he stopped before the kiln and thrust his head inside. Then he turned back.

'What're you doing around here, hey?' he barked.

The boy was struck with fear. He felt like taking to his heels.

'What're you standing there stuck for, hey?' shouted Jumali.

'Hassan Bey sent me,' stammered Mustafa. 'To help you . . .'

With surprising agility Jumali swung his heavy frame impatiently back to the kiln.

'Now that's fine!' he growled. 'What does Hassan Bey think he's doing, sending along a child not bigger than the palm of your hand?' He flung his hand out. 'Not bigger than this hand! You go right back and tell him to find someone else.'

Mustafa was dumb with dismay. He took a few wavering steps towards the town. Then he stopped. The white trousers danced before his eyes. He wanted to cry.

'Uncle Jumali,' he begged weakly, 'I'll work harder than a grown man . . .'

'Listen to the pup! Do you know what it means to fire a kiln?'

'Oh yes . . .'

'Why, you little bastard, three days, three nights of feeding wood into this hole you see here, taking it in turns, you and I . . .'

'I know, I know!'

'Listen to the little bastard! Did you learn all this in your mother's womb? Now bugger off and stop pestering me.

Mustafa had a flash of inspiration.

'I can't go back,' he said. 'Hassan Bey paid me in advance and I've already spent the money.'

'Go away!' shouted Jumali. 'You'll get me into trouble.'

Mustafa rebelled.

'But why? Why d'you want to take the bread out of my mouth? Just because I'm a child . . . I can work as hard as anyone.' Suddenly he ran up to Jumali and grasped his hand. 'I swear it, Uncle Jumali! You'll see how I'll feed that kiln. Anyway, I've spent the pay . . .'

'Well, all right,' Jumali said at last. 'We'll see . . .'

He lit a stick of pinewood and thrust it in. The wood crackled and a long tongue of flame spurted out.

'Damn!' he cursed. 'Filled it up to bursting, they have, the bastards! Everything they do is wrong.'

Still cursing, he gave Mustafa a few instructions. Then he lit a cigarette and moved off into the shade of a fig-tree.

When the flames that were lapping the mouth of the kiln had receded, Mustafa picked up an armful of brushwood and threw it in. Then another . . . And another . . .

The dusty road, the thick-spreading fig-trees, the stream that flowed like molten tin, the ashen sky, the lone bird flapping by, the scorched grass, the small wilting yellow flowers, the whole world drooped wearily under the impact of the noonday heat. Mustafa's face was as red as the flames, his shirt dripping, as he ran carrying the brushwood from the heat of the sun to the heat of the kiln.

At the close of the sizzling afternoon, little white clouds rise up in clusters far off in the south over the Mediterranean, heralding the cool moist breeze that will soon enwrap the heat-baked creatures as in a wet soothing towel. As the first fresh puff of wind stirred up the dust on the road, Jumali

called to Mustafa from where he lay supine in the heavy
shade of the fig-tree.

'Hey, boy, come along and let's eat!'

Mustafa was quivering with exhaustion and hunger.

Hassan Bey had provided Jumali with a bundle of food.
There was white cheese, green onions and wafer-bread. They
fell to without a word. The sun sank down behind the poplar
trees that stood out like a dark curtain against the glow.
Mustafa picked up the jug and went to the stream. The
water tasted like warm blood. They drank it thirstily.
Jumali wiped his long moustache with the back of his hand.

'I'm going to sleep a while, Mustafa,' he said. 'Wake me
up when you're tired, eh?'

It was long past midnight. The moon had dropped behind the wall of poplars. Mustafa's thin sweating face
shone red in the blaze. He threw in an armful of wood and
watched the wild onrush of flames swallow it up. There was
a loud crackling at first, then a long, long moaning sound
that was almost human.

Like a baby crying its heart out, he thought.

'Are you tired? D'you want me?' came Jumali's sleepy
voice.

A tremor shook his body. He felt a cold sweat breaking
out all over him.

'Oh no, Uncle Jumali!' he cried. 'I never get tired. You
go on sleeping.'

He could not bear to go near the kiln any more. Now he
heaped as much wood as possible close to the opening and
shoved it in with the long wooden fork. Then, backing
before the sudden surge of heat, he scrambled on to a mound
near by and stood awhile against the night breeze. But the
air bore down, heavy and stifling, drowning him.

There is a bird that sings just before the break of dawn. A very tiny bird. Its call is long-drawn and piercing. He heard the bird's call and saw a widening ribbon of light brighten up the sky behind the hill.

Just then Jumali woke up.

'Are you tired?' he asked.

'No . . . No . . . I'm not tired . . .' But his voice broke, strangling with tears.

Jumali rose and stretched himself.

'Go and sleep a little now,' he said.

He was asleep when Hassan Bey arrived.

'How's the boy doing?' he asked. 'Working all right?'

Jumali's lips curled.

'A chit of a child . . .' he said.

'Well, you'll have to shift along as best you can. I'll make it worth your while,' said Hassan Bey as he left.

When Mustafa awoke the sun was heaving down upon him and the earth was like red-hot iron. His bones ached as though they had been pounded in a mortar. Setting his teeth, he struggled up and ran to the kiln.

'Uncle Jumali,' he faltered, 'I'm sorry I slept so long . . .'

'I told you you'd never make it,' said Jumali sourly.

Mustafa did not answer. He scraped up some brushwood and began feeding the kiln. After a while he felt a little better.

Hurray! he thought. We've weathered the first day.

But the two huge searing days loomed before him and the stifling clamminess of the infernal nights. He chased the thought away and conjured up the image of the white trousers . . .

The last night . . . The moon bright over the poplar trees . . .

'Wake me up if you get tired,' says Jumali . . .

The fire has to be kept up at the same level or the bricks will not bake and a whole two days' work will have been in vain. The flames must flare out greedily licking at the night. The hated flames . . . He has not the strength to reach the refreshing mound any longer. He can only throw himself on the ground and let the moist coolness of the earth seep into his body. But always the fear in his heart that sleep will overcome him . . .

His eyes were clinging to the east, groping for the ribbon of light. But it was pitch dark and Jumali snored on loudly.

Damn you, Uncle Jumali! Damn you . . .

Suddenly, the whole world started trembling. The dark curtain of poplars, the hills, the flames, the kiln were turning round and round. He was going to vomit.

'Jumali! Uncle Jumali . . .'

He had fainted.

It was a good while before Jumali called again in his drowsy voice.

'Are you tired, Mustafa?'

There was no answer. Then he caught sight of the darkened kiln. He rushed up and fetched the child a furious kick.

'You've done for me, you little bastard! They'll make me pay for the bricks now . . .'

He peered into the opening and took hope. A few small flames were still wavering against the inner wall.

Mustafa came to as the dawn was breaking. His heart quaked at the sight of Jumali, his hairy chest bared, stoking the kiln.

'Uncle Jumali,' he faltered, 'really, I never meant to . . .'

Jumali cast an angry glance over his shoulder.

'Shut up, damn you! Go to hell!'

Mustafa hung his head and sat there motionless until the sun rose over the hill. Then he fell asleep in the same position.

A brick kiln is large and spacious, rather like a well that has been capped with a dome. When it is first set alight the bricks take on a leaden hue. The second day, they turn a dull black. But on the morning of the third day, they are a fiery red . . .

Mustafa awoke with fear in his heart. The sun was quarter high and Hassan Bey was standing near the kiln. The bricks were sparkling like red crystal.

'Well, my boy?' Hassan Bey laughed. 'So we came here to sleep, did we?'

'Uncle, I swear that every night . . .'

Jumali threw him a dour look. He dared not go on.

They sealed up the mouth of the kiln.

The cobbler had shaggy eyebrows and a beard. His back was slightly hunched. The shop, dusty and cobwebby, smelled of leather and rawhide.

A week had gone by and still no sign of Hassan Bey. Mustafa was eating his heart out with anxiety, but he said nothing. Then one day Hassan Bey happened to pass before the shop.

'Hey, Hassan!' the cobbler called. 'When are you going to pay the lad here?'

Hassan Bey hesitated. Then he took a one-lira note and two twenty-five kurush coins and placed them on the bench.

'Here you are,' he said.

The cobbler stared at the money.

'But that's only a lira and a half. The child worked three days . . .'

'Well, he slept all the time, so I paid his share to Jumali.

This, I'm giving him simply out of consideration for you,' said Hassan Bey, turning to leave.

'Uncle, I swear that every night . . .' began Mustafa, but his voice stuck in his throat. He lowered his head.

There was a long, painful silence.

'Look, Mustafa,' said the cobbler at last, 'you're more than an apprentice now. You patch soles really well. From now on you'll get a lira a week for your work.'

Mustafa raised his head slowly. His eyes were shining through the tears.

'Take these five liras,' said the cobbler, 'and give them to the tailor Vayis with my compliments. Tell him to cut your white trousers out of the best material he's got. With the rest of the money you can buy your shoes. I'm taking this fellow's money, so you owe me only three and a half weeks' pay . . .'

Mustafa laughed with glee.

In those days the blue five-lira note carried the picture of a wolf, its tongue hanging out as it galloped swift as the wind.

The Drumming-out

It was three months now that the district had been without a Commissioner. Resul Efendi, the clerk, had been appointed deputy, but as far as the rice-planters were concerned he might as well not have existed. To them he was only a silly old fool, too frightened of his own shadow to sign a single rice-sowing permit. April was upon them and applications for sowing were piling in. The usual renting of fields, the disputes over irrigation conduits, the swapping and selling, the cheating and conning were in full swing. But all Resul Efendi did was to repeat, 'I won't get mixed up in this rice business. Not even if it costs me my post, I won't! Not on your life!' Resul Efendi was not born yesterday. He had had trouble over the rice-sowing before, and this time there was that land which Okchuoglu wanted to plant although the village of Sazlidere was right in the middle of it. If he issued a permit for that, he would come by at least twenty thousand liras. As simple as that, yes, but the rice-planters would give him no peace once they had got him where they wanted him. Resul Efendi valued his peace and quiet and had always made it a rule to avoid stepping on a rotten board if he could help it. He well knew that dealing with those devilish rice-planters was like rousing a hornet's nest.

The worst of them was Murtaza Agha, an out-and-out rascal, always after Resul Efendi like the plague.

'So, Resul Efendi!' he would buttonhole him on every occasion, 'we hear you're snapping your fingers at the Rice Commission? Not signing a single permit, eh? That won't do, Resul Efendi! You and I used to be such good friends, but now there's no Commissioner you think you can put on hoity-toity airs, eh?'

Resul Efendi would bow very low and bestow on Murtaza Agha the same warm smile he always had for everyone.

'What can I do, Agha? Much obliged to you,' he would murmur and, raising his hat courteously, go on his way.

'Eh, Resul Efendi!' the other would shout after him. 'You with your disarming ways and innocent manners! That's how you try to take the wind out of our sails.'

Resul Efendi would turn and doff his hat again. 'Much obliged to you, Agha,' he would repeat and walk on.

April was coming to a close and still no sign of the new Commissioner. The Rice Commission held meeting after meeting, but wild horses would not have dragged Resul Efendi there. The documents were brought to him, but he would not even touch them. He had to contend with the enraged rice-planters night and day now.

'Please, please,' he would beg woefully, 'please don't do this to me, Aghas. You're all great powerful men. What do you want from poor old Resul, who's only got a year and a half till his pension? Don't drag me into this. The new Commissioner will be here any day now.'

But one day the rice-planters went so far that the mild, good-tempered Resul Efendi flew off the handle.

'I resign!' he shouted. 'I've had enough of you, you devils. You've made me wish I were dead. I resign!'

He sat down at once to compose his letter of resignation and wrote five full pages of typescript that would have made anyone's heart bleed. Fortunately for him, the Commander of the Gendarmerie and the other officials talked him out of sending it in. Resul Efendi closed his eyes and solemnly tore up the letter. Suddenly, like lightning, he had a vision of his resignation being accepted, of himself without a job, without a penny in the world. A wave of dizziness passed over him and a bitter emptiness froze his heart.

Meanwhile, complaints about Resul Efendi poured over the wires to Ankara and Adana, accusing him of corruption, of dishonesty, of immorality. His wife was a whore, he had sold his daughter, he drank night and day and held loud wassails in the Commissioner's office. Before sending off these telegrams, the Postmaster took a copy of each and read it out to all comers, so that the whole town knew them by heart and they were repeated all over the place. But still there was no reaction either from Ankara or the county seat of Adana. Obviously, such telegrams were nothing new in government quarters. Nobody paid any attention.

The hot weather sets in in April. As the yellow, red, mauve and white flowers sprout from the earth, as the world gleams, washed and purified, in a bright green freshness, the heat suddenly bears down on the Chukurova plain.

Resul Efendi would leave his office in the evening and make straight for home. For thirty years he had never deviated from his course. His house was surrounded by a high-walled yard in which stood five tall, dark-leaved eucalyptus trees. A mosaic path of pebbles ran from the gate to the house, which was painted pink. Over the front door, the skull of a horse decorated with blue beads, garlic and pine-cones had been hung against the evil eye. Snow-white curtains fluttered in the windows. As soon as Resul Efendi raised his hand to the knocker, before he had even lowered it, the door would quickly open. He would smile his warmest, his most childlike smile. Resul Efendi's wife, like himself, was small and slightly built. She wore a spotless white kerchief over her head. Her front teeth were very large and protruding, but for some reason, perhaps because of her huge dark eyes, this did not spoil her face. She would stand aside in affectionate respect, saying, 'Welcome home, Resul Efendi,' and follow one pace behind him as he walked leisurely towards the house. He would stop on the porch, take off his shoes, pull a chair under him and stretch out his legs. Then she would wash and rub his feet, sometimes for as long as an hour. His nineteen-year-old daughter would come down, a tall girl with black brows and dark eyes, always dressed with an eye to the latest fashion. 'Good-evening, Father,' she would greet him, and Resul Efendi would lift up his head and smile.

This time the courtyard gate opened before he could raise his hand to the knocker, but he hardly saw his wife. Only a vague whiteness floated before his eyes. He did not even hear her voice. He walked in and, without stopping on the porch, without taking off his shoes, he went upstairs and flung himself weakly on the sofa.

'What's the matter, Resul Efendi?' cried his wife anxiously. 'Are you ill?'

He rested his head against the whitewashed wall, closing his eyes.

'What is it?'

His lips moved slightly: 'They say I'm going to be removed. All those telegrams . . . Ah, it's the end for us!'

'Ah, the devils!' wailed his wife. 'They want to ruin us. They want to make beggars of us. Ah, the fiends . . .'

Resul Efendi's face was white and cold as marble.

'What hurts most,' he murmured in a dead voice, 'is that we haven't been able to live one full year in our new house. That's what's killing me. But hush, Hanum, hush. Allah is generous . . .'

'Aaah!' she lamented. 'The blood-suckers! How can they do such a thing?' Tears poured from her eyes.

It was ten years now that, sick of moving from one rented, tumbledown, bug-ridden house to another, Resul Efendi had purchased this small plot of land. A year later he was able to buy the stone. The third year he secured the timber and the fourth the zinc sheets for the roof. The actual building began in the fifth year. Finally, in the tenth year, the pink-wash was laid on and, happy as kings, the family moved in. For months, husband and wife talked about nothing but their new home. One window would engross them for days. The mere placing of a flower-pot became an important issue. And then Resul Efendi was appointed Deputy Commissioner. At first they were delighted. But it was not long before they found themselves plunged in the rice-planting intrigues, and from that day onwards an atmosphere of mourning enveloped their beloved home.

Matters had now come to a crisis for the desperate rice-planters and, since the telegrams had produced no results, they resorted to threats. One day, as Resul Efendi was coming home from the office, he was waylaid by Murtaza Agha.

'Look here, you rat, the money I've poured into my land is worth the life of a hundred dogs like you! You'd better stick your dirty name on those papers, and fast! I'm not going to see my fortune go down the drain because of you. And get this straight, Resul Efendi, a bullet costs only fifty kurush.'

Resul Efendi's head whirled.

'But Agha,' he murmured helplessly, 'what have I done to you?'

'What more can you do, you snake-in-the-grass?' roared Murtaza Agha. 'I'll have no rice crop this year, if this goes on.'

'Yes, yes, of course . . . Much obliged to you, Agha.'

He knew this was no vain threat. Murtaza Agha had a good number of murders to his credit and he had got away with every single one of them, even the time when he had baited that fatal trap for the gendarme officer, Shukru Bey. The words 'fifty kurush' went whizzing round his head like a bullet. After that, he locked and double-locked his door at night. He placed sandbags in the windows and even in the chimney, in case they might throw a bomb down it. He hardly slept for nights on end.

The good news found him a bag of skin and bones. He read the document again and again, unable to trust his eyes. He took it to the registration clerk and had him read it, just to make sure. Then, carefully folding the paper, he put it in his pocket and made for home at a run, although office hours were not yet over. This was certainly the first time such a thing had happened in thirty years. Resul Efendi in the streets during office hours, and running too! The towns-people's eyes almost popped out of their heads. For years he had come and gone along the same street with the same measured step and the same greeting for everyone. Why, he had almost trod in the same footsteps!

He had to knock three times before the door opened.

'Who is it?' his wife called out anxiously.

'It's me,' answered Resul Efendi, trembling with excitement.

She unlocked the door and stood staring. Resul Efendi was smiling at her, his own sweet, familiar smile. He walked in, still smiling, took off his shoes on the porch and stretched out his feet towards the basin, a thing he had not done for days. She curbed her curiosity and set about washing his feet.

'Look at this, Hanum,' he said at last. Slowly he took the letter out of his pocket and read it out to her.

'Allah be praised!' she exclaimed. 'To think I should see this day! Thanks be to Allah . . .'

Resul Efendi kept repeating the new Commissioner's name like a litany.

'Fikret Irmakli! Fikret Bey . . . Just out of school . . . This is his first post. Fikret Irmakli! Fikret Bey . . . So young . . . Fikret Irmakli . . .'

II

The best house in the town belonged to Long Rahmet, a rice-planter. It had created quite a stir while it was being built the previous year, and when it was finished people came from all over the country to look at it. No other house would do for the new Commissioner. This was a matter of life and death, and Kemal Tashan decided to take on the task of furnishing it properly. This young man, a graduate from the Agricultural College, who had worked as a government official for a span and then resigned, had made a fortune out of rice in the last couple of years. The most expensively dressed man in town and a good talker, he knew how to air clouds of high-sounding phrases to good effect.

The Commissioner was a bachelor, but he was bound to marry some time. So Kemal Tashan put in a double bed with a quilt of real down. As for the carpets, he waved aside the cheap local ones and bought expensive Persian rugs. He even hung pictures on the walls, more than a dozen of them, setting all the other Aghas agape.

'This is just right for our young Commissioner,' gloated Murtaza Agha, licking his thick lips. 'I wouldn't have done better for my own son!'

Once the newcomer was settled in this bower of bliss, he would be in the bag. Murtaza Agha knew by experience that it could not be otherwise. Any man, so long as he was young, could be made a cat's-paw, and young administrative officers like this made the best cat's-paws in the world.

Although only ten days had passed since the news of the Commissioner's appointment, everyone in town already knew all there was to know about him, where he was born, who his mother and father were, his financial position, what sort of student he had been at school, if he had a weakness for women, if he drank and how much, his likes and dislikes, every single thing. They had even managed to lay hands on a photograph of him.

There were fourteen cars in the town and more were brought in for the occasion. A couple of buses were found, and cars and buses were decked with flags and flowers. Two drummers and two pipers were engaged. A delegation of notables was chosen to meet the Commissioner, and at five o'clock on a Friday the Aghas and the officials, all dressed in their very best, piled into the cars. The young men of the town were packed into the buses and told to keep cheering. The drummers, perched on top of the buses, started drumming away, and with a great cheer they all set out.

At the Jeyhan railway station the cars were lined up in order of precedence. The first one, which almost disappeared under heaps of flowers, was a brand-new Chrysler model. At last the train bearing the Commissioner steamed into the station. Kemal Tashan was on his toes. He beckoned to two of his men and leaped on to the step. He had the Commissioner's photograph in his hand. In a second-class compartment he spotted a young man whose long, straight hair kept falling over his light-brown eyes and whose lips were a thin compressed line in a long pale face with black eyebrows. The young man was trying to pull his suitcases down from the rack where they were jammed among baskets and bundles. His trousers were creased and his face and shirt rather grimy. Kemal Tashan glanced at the photograph and stepped forward.

'Please, Beyefendi, please!' he said. 'Let the men take them.'

'It's all right,' said the young man, rather surprised.

'But the men are here for that, Beyefendi,' smiled Kemal Tashan. He held out his hand. 'I'm Kemal Tashan, one of the town notables, by profession a farmer. We've come to welcome you.'

The young man looked bewildered.

'I'm honoured, I'm sure. My name's Fikret Irmakli. This is a lot of trouble . . . Thank you. Thank you very much.'

He was full of apprehension. What had he not heard about these Anatolian towns! A cluster of mud huts lost in the vastness of the endless steppe, buried under snow in winter, smothered with dust in summer . . . The loneliness . . . The conflicts with all-powerful Aghas and bandits . . . The town notables he had always pictured as men with shiny boots and breeches, and coiling moustachios, each armed with a pistol or a dagger . . . But this Kemal Tashan, with his young, glowing, clear-cut features that inspired confidence, was a notable . . . Somehow he reminded him of Nuzhet, his closest friend at the School of Political Science. They had the same smile.

His amazement increased still further when he saw the crowd that had come to greet him. Five hundred persons, young and old, were lined up like soldiers, facing the train.

'This way, please,' Kemal Tashan was saying. 'This way, Beyefendi.'

The Commissioner's eyes filled with tears. Ah, the humble people of Anatolia, he thought, hospitable, noble, long-suffering, brave . . . What an honour to be called to serve such a people! To sleep like them along with the animals in the stables . . . To eat the same things . . . To be eaten up by mosquitoes like them . . . What an honour!

Kemal Tashan was introducing everyone in turn.

'Murtaza Agha, farmer and notable. Okchuoglu Bey, farmer and notable . . .'

He shook their hands with fervour.

'How do you do? This is a great honour. How do you do?'

'Mustafa Patir, farmer and notable . . .'

'How do you do?'

'Emin Chelik, one of our biggest farmers. Sheref Horozlu . . .'

His emotion increased as he shook hands with everyone. To all, even to the drummers, he said 'How do you do?' in the same vibrant tones.

Then, the Commissioner in front and the crowd following, they went out to the cars. Kemal Tashan and Murtaza Agha made a rush for the flower-decked car, bumping into each other in their haste. It was Murtaza Agha who succeeded in getting hold of the door.

'Please step in, Beyefendi,' he cried, bending his tall figure in an obsequious bow. 'Our own Commissioner! Our dear Commissioner!'

'Not at all . . . Please!' protested the Commissioner, embarrassed.

All the while the young men were cheering away loudly.

'Long live the Commissioner! Long live the Commissioner!'

On the Commissioner's right sat Murtaza Agha. On his left Kemal Tashan. It was some time before the Commissioner was able to pull himself together. He tossed back the long lock of hair that fell over his forehead.

'Please excuse me. I seem to have lost my tongue. I'm so excited. So surprised . . . In Istanbul we've always been told that Anatolia is hell, that Anatolian town notables are so many monsters. But here I see . . . Are these gentlemen really the notables?'

'Yes, Beyefendi, we're the notables,' laughed Kemal Tashan.

'I've heard,' continued the Commissioner, 'that malaria is rampant in this district. Thousands of people die of it every year, especially children. I had a letter about it.'

'Those sneaking communists, Blind Jemal and Pehlivan Usta, sent it, I'll wager,' broke out Murtaza Agha angrily. 'They've always been against us.'

Kemal Tashan hastened to cover Murtaza Agha's imprudent line of talk.

'Ah, Beyefendi,' he said. 'There are deaths . . . But the standard of living's so low! When you see how the peasants live, right in the marshes, in reed huts, animals and all crowded into one single room, you'll wonder they don't all die . . . For food they have only boiled bulgur and bread. And at the end of the winter they eat grass because there's nothing left. They boil the grass and eat it! As a luxury they have a little watery yoghurt. It's a miracle they keep alive at all!'

The Commissioner was staring at Kemal Tashan, his eyes wide with pain.

'And the malaria on top of all this . . .' he said.

Murtaza Agha fidgeted. 'Those heathenish communists, Blind Jemal and Pehlivan Usta,' he muttered. 'It was their letter, damn them . . .'

'People exaggerate, Commissioner,' continued Kemal Tashan smoothly. 'There is malaria, of course, but certainly not as much as in the old days. In fact it's gradually being wiped out. We're helping the villagers to take precautions.'

The sun was sinking as they reached the bridge that spanned the river just outside the town. Hundreds of men, women and children were crowded there, waiting. They were strangely silent. The Commissioner waved at them, but they only stared at the flower-decked car with vacant eyes. He was disquieted.

Immediately after crossing the bridge, they entered the town. Poor reed huts were huddled on the left, and on the right stood the large, ugly, whitewashed houses of the notables. They drove through the market-place with its broken cobbles and stopped at the town club which had been humming with expectancy for the past two hours. 'The sowing season's as good as past, and not a single permit's out yet. Let's hope to God this Commissioner's not going to be nosy, checking the field plans and all that . . .'

People assailed Murtaza Agha with questions. He waxed enthusiastic.

'He's not one of those upstarts like that little rat Resul,' he said, 'he's a real man. "Agha," he said to me, "I never expected to meet anyone like you out here. Why, you're a man after my own heart! To think they sent me an insulting letter about you!" And who'd do that, my friends, but those communists, Blind Jemal and Pehlivan Usta? "But," he said, "as soon as I saw you I realized what was what." Ah, he's a noble soul, our Commissioner. And not surprising, too. Why, he was born in Istanbul, the city of the Sultans! Murtaza Agha'll give his soul for him, make him rich, make him a lord! Has anybody come to harm who's leaned on Murtaza Agha?'

A banquet for a hundred persons had been laid out at Nazif's Restaurant, and again the Commissioner was seated between Kemal Tashan and Murtaza Agha. At the other end of the table sat Tewfik Ali Bey, once a lawyer and now one of the rich rice Aghas. Glasses were raised again and again to the health of the Commissioner and to the health of the town. Then Tewfik Ali Bey could contain himself no longer. He clambered on to his chair and embarked on a fervent speech. On and one he talked about the War of Independence and the invaluable services he and his friends had rendered the country, of how they had driven the enemy out of this sacred portion of Turkish soil, of how he himself had planted a park for the town when he was mayor. Then he came to the Commissioner, and expatiated on the town's great luck in having such a young, energetic, courageous and patriotic administrator. He ended his speech by saluting the Commissioner with a broad flourish of the hand from lips to forehead. Then he stepped heavily off his chair.

The Commissioner felt bound to say a few words. Slightly drunk, he rose and spoke of his joy at the prospect of serving the warm-hearted people of this beautiful town. He had felt himself drawn in brotherly affection to them all from the minute he had set foot here, and so it would be until the end of his life. His voice strangled with emotion and he sat down.

This speech was punctuated by ecstatic exclamations from Murtaza Agha, who was half-seas over. 'The apple of my eye, that's what you are, my Commissioner! I'd give my soul for you, my brave lad . . .'

The gathering ended in an effusion of general good feeling, but the Commissioner's head was spinning. The dusty road, the flower-decked car, the cordial welcome by those dreaded town notables who had turned out to be such kindly, hospitable people . . . The long, lonely poplar trees on the road . . . Himself and Nermin on the eve of his departure strolling together under the shady arch of the great trees that bordered Dolmabahche Palace . . . Everything was swimming in his mind. He had never been out of Istanbul, and she had spoken to him of the tall, desolate, ever-swaying poplars that for her embodied all the melancholy of the vast central Anatolian steppe. Before them lay the dark blue waters of the Bosphorus and the leaping waves . . . Behind, glittering cars flashing by on the shady road, and the little square alive with hundreds of pigeons . . . And across on the Asiatic side of the Bosphorus, Scutari and his own neat home . . . His mother, with her white headkerchief, her large blue eyes and her long pale hands . . . Her white linen, smelling fragrantly of soap . . . The fig-trees of Scutari with their deep, heavy shade . . . And right on the shore Sinan's tiny, gem-like mosque, and the children playing hopscotch in its courtyard . . .

He lay awake till dawn and, as the first rays of light appeared at his window, his thoughts strayed to Nermin's father, Husnu Bey. What was it he had said, what was it, as he twisted his long curling moustache? 'My boy,' he had said, 'don't let yourself be deceived by appearances. Men are two-faced.' Who knows, he thought, as he tossed restlessly on his bed. Husnu Bey must be mistaken. All these notables for instance . . .

He got out of bed and stood staring at the pictures on the wall. Then he smiled. Small-town taste . . . They were not likely to hang a Picasso. But what a fine house it was. It even had a bath of green porcelain. He slipped under the shower, shivering.

It was exactly ten minutes to nine when he left the house. The servant had laid the table for breakfast, but he did not give it a glance. He never ate breakfast.

A bright sunshine flooded the town as he walked to his

office along gardens planted with olive trees. Resul Efendi
was at the door, bent double in low bows.

'Good-morning, Beyefendi. Welcome. Your room is this
way . . .'

The furniture consisted of a worm-eaten desk, a dirty
chair shining greasily and a torn armchair with its springs
sticking out. He was taken aback.

'Is this the Commissioner's room?' He frowned.

'Yes, Beyefendi.'

He went to the desk and sat down. His head was aching
slightly.

Resul Efendi stood before him, still bowing.

'I'm very grateful to you, Beyefendi,' he blurted out at
last. 'Very, very much indebted to you . . .'

The Commissioner did not try to understand. Since
alighting from the train, he had been showered with such
extraordinary attentions that he took this for just another
compliment.

All that day, the officials, the Aghas, the town notables, the
doctors and lawyers, the Muhtars and the more prominent
villagers called to pay their respects. The office buzzed like
a beehive until evening. The Commissioner was bemused.
At lunch and at dinner the town notables still stuck to him.
His thoughts were no longer clear. He went to bed early and
fell asleep at once.

The next morning he woke up, refreshed and cheerful.
He wandered about the house, whistling an air from
Beethoven's Ninth Symphony. The sun was shining over
the olive trees under his window. In the distance, the river,
a bright silver ribbon coiling across the plain, seemed to soar
into the air above the melting waves of mist. A luminous
stream of happiness gushed within him. He wanted to em-

brace the whole world, its earth and stones, its silvery olive trees and twittering sparrows, its every creature.

He shaved and had a bath, then went out. Still whistling the Ninth Symphony, he passed through the market-place with friendly greetings to all the shopkeepers. The office did not seem to him as miserable as the day before. He saw neither the dirt on the chairs nor the worm-holes on the desk.

The Agricultural Technician brought in a number of files.

'You've arrived just in time, Beyefendi,' he said. 'The applications for rice-sowing have been piling in so . . . There's a meeting of the Rice Commission today. Of course you will preside . . .'

He opened the files and produced plans and sketches. The Commissioner did not understand a thing.

'All right,' he said, glancing through them cursorily. 'We'll settle this at the meeting.'

The Commission consisted of the Excise Officer, the Health Inspector, the Agricultural Technician, a representative of the rice-planters, and the Commissioner. The rice-planters had long ago circumvented the scruples of the Health Inspector and the Agricultural Technician, and their representative on the Commission was Kemal Tashan. It was he who explained the plans and sketches to the Commissioner. The permits had been drawn up weeks ago. The Commissioner signed a few of them and put off the rest until a second meeting.

That evening, Okchuoglu made his appearance at the club. A tall, broad-shouldered man of fifty, sporting riding-boots and a huge moustache, he ambled up to the table where the Commissioner was sitting, heatedly discussing with Kemal Tashan the problems of the nation and the remedies to its ills, while the government doctor, who had felt drawn to the

Commissioner from the first, listened to them, smiling. With a ponderous greeting Okchuoglu joined them, but for a long time maintained a solemn silence. This was in the best tradition of the old feudal lords for, as the saying goes, a firm rock never moves. So, all the descendants of feudal families made it a point to be chary of their speech. Sitting stiff as pokers and with grave, unsmiling faces, they would listen to what was said, nodding occasionally. Okchuoglu had been nodding his head for quite a while now.

'Commissioner, Kemal Bey, Doctor,' he said at last, 'I'm inviting you all to Adana this evening. My car's ready outside.'

The Commissioner looked at Kemal Tashan.

'All right, Okchuoglu,' said Kemal Tashan, 'we won't refuse you.'

'Thank you, but I have some work to do,' said the doctor.

'Nonsense, Doctor!' cried Okchuoglu in his deep voice.

Kemal Tashan leaned over to the doctor. 'You must come, Doctor,' he whispered. 'He's obtained the permit for his land at Sazlidere, so he's in a fine mood for spending. Let's make the most of it.'

In the car Okchuoglu became expansive.

'Yes, this country, this land of paradise for which we'd all give our souls, is backward and underdeveloped . . . But it'll progress. It's changing already. Just think! Before we introduced rice-growing, the land here was only a swamp. The peasants would go begging for a bite of bread! As for rice, they'd never had a grain of the stuff in their guts. Now in every house you see a huge sack of rice. Rice has brought life to this country. Do you know people here had never even seen a mosquito-net?' He roared with laughter. 'I remember once, in the early days, I was staying the night at a village and had just spread out my mosquito-net, when there was a great commotion all around me. The whole village, men, women, children, old and sick, were gathered there, gaping. So I explained to them the uses of the mosquito-net. Now, everyone sleeps under nets. They've learnt to protect themselves . . .'

The Commissioner was whistling the tune from the Ninth Symphony. The wind rushed by smelling of dust and dried grass and marsh, as the car glided swiftly over the flat, silvered plain. Soon they would be enjoying themselves in one of the most expensive night-clubs of Adana . . .

III

Sazlidere was right in the middle of Okchuoglu's one thousand five hundred acres, and under the malaria regulations rice cultivation was prohibited in the four hundred acres immediately surrounding the village. But the minute Okchuoglu had set eyes on the young Commissioner his heart had given a bound. He had rushed straight to the Agricultural Technician.

'Look here, my friend, we're in luck with this new Commissioner. Let's have a new plan drawn up to include the village. Tear up the old one, and be quick for God's sake!'

The other smiled. 'So you've sized him up, have you?'

And so Okchuoglu had got his permit according to the new plan. But that was not enough. The fields belonging to the village had to be rented, the cotton, sesame and vegetables to be bought and the villagers to be kept quiet. And time was running short.

Okchuoglu was the kind of man who would not for a million have spent more than an hour in any village. However, for three days now he had not emerged from Sazlidere, a sure sign that he had struck a bad patch. The whole of

Sazlidere belonged to Osman Agha, a quiet, mild-tempered man who could not say boo to a goose. All the sixty families in the village share-cropped for him. Osman Agha was tractable enough, but the peasants were making a nuisance of themselves, especially those confounded Kurds, who once they had got something into their heads would rather have their throats cut than yield an inch. And now, egged on by Memed Ali, that scourge of Allah who could not even speak Turkish properly, they were obviously out to give Okchuoglu a hard time.

In the village coffee-house with its trellised awning of brushwood and branches, a fuming Okchuoglu, switching his boots with his silver-handled whip and chewing one end of his long moustache, faced the recalcitrant peasants. He had tried everything, wiles and threats and oaths, and now the last straw he clung to was the Commissioner.

'You people don't know this Commissioner yet,' he was saying. 'A fine upstanding young man, God bless him, energetic, courageous and only twenty-six! Shall I tell you what he said to me at the night-club? "Why," he said, "with a crop like rice in our hands, a crop that yields eighty to one, a hundred to one, a crop that can bring in millions, this district should become a paradise on earth. Rice is a national crop," he said, "a noble crop. Growing rice is just as patriotic as going to war. Because," he said, "if you don't grow rice, what will our soldiers eat who are spilling their blood for our sake on this nation's borders? What will you all eat?" Yes, that's what he said. But you peasants can't understand this. Oh no! It's, oh dear, a mosquito's bitten me, or, oh dear, the malaria's killing us! Always complaining ... "I know these peasants," the Commissioner said to me. "I know what a damned nuisance they can be. Their minds are incapable of grasping these delicate national matters. That's why," he said, "I take no notice of all these irrigation regulations. The national crop is much more important to me than a few paltry laws." I like these young officials, bless them. Real patriots, they are! He said to me in Adana: "If there were ten villages in a rice-producing area, I'd still get rid of the lot." That's what our great administrators say. But a twopenny-halfpenny peasant comes along and complains of mosquitoes and malaria! Of course we have to put up with mosquitoes and malaria in the interest of this national crop! Has anyone ever seen a rose without a thorn? . . .'

For days now the village had been afire with alarming rumours. It was said that Okchuoglu had lavishly fêted the Commissioner in the night-clubs of Adana, that he had wangled the illegal permit out of him with a fifty-thousand-lira bribe, that they were on the best of terms . . . The peasants had no illusions. Time and again they had stood by helpless while Okchuoglu twisted officials round his little finger.

Osman Agha was a short, sickly man with a red, pock-marked face. He was clad in faded black shalvar-trousers and a striped vest.

'Agha,' he said stretching out his scraggy, reddish neck, 'you know best, of course, but the village will be flooded. I can always go up to my place in the hills, but what are the others to do?'

'Didn't you rent me your fields, with a contract and all?' asked Okchuoglu.

'Yes . . .'

'Well then?'

Osman Agha bowed his head.

'You know best, Agha . . .'

Okchuoglu started to walk up and down, lashing his boots.

'Look, my friends, I'm offering to buy up your cotton and sesame before they're ripe. All you have to do is to sell the crops to me as you always do, but this time right away. That's all!'

'And if we don't?' asked Memed Ali the Kurd.

Okchuoglu stopped dead. Memed Ali was not a man to be easily cowed. He had been a notorious bandit in the Taurus mountains, but after the general amnesty in 1933 he had come down from the mountains and had settled at Sazlidere.

The memory of the old bandit flashed through Okchuoglu's mind. He tried to smile.

'Oh well, Memed Ali, do as you like. Your field can remain there like a flower in the middle of the rice-paddies.' He turned to the others. 'Thirty liras the dunum for the cotton and thirty for the sesame. Fifty for the vegetables. No hoeing, no harvesting, no work at all for you!'

'That's very good of you, Agha,' said a villager. 'But how are we going to live here? We know it's very kind of you to give us all that money. But six months in a swamp! Six whole months in hot mud! And the malaria . . .'

'Thirty liras the dunum,' repeated Okchuoglu. 'Thirty! And you won't have done a thing to earn it. Just scattered a few seeds on Osman's land. Do you think I'm doing this for love? Does a man in his right senses pay thirty liras a dunum for cotton that's hardly sprouted yet? I'm giving you this money because of the swamp and the mosquitoes and the malaria.'

'But Agha, it's not one day or two. Six whole months! How can we live in mud for that long?'

'Look here, I've rented this land and I've a right to flood it. My offer to you is pure kindness. If you don't get out, I'll flood the land all the same.'

'There's law!' protested Memed Ali the Kurd. 'Law says

partial irrigation for fields five hundred metres from village.
You give water ten days and cut it forty-eight hours so field
dries. And then law says continuous irrigation for fields
three thousand metres from village . . .'

Okchuoglu went and sat down under the awning. He was
streaming with sweat.

'That's Kurdish sense for you!' he sneered. 'God help us
when they get something into their heads! Partial irrigation, continuous irrigation! For the love of God, tell me,
can't mosquitoes travel three thousand metres? Didn't they
reach you last year all the way from my rice-paddy below
Oksuzlu, not three but ten thousand metres away? As for
cutting off the water for two days, why, there are swamps
around here that wouldn't dry in a year!' He turned to
Memed Ali. 'You'd better send a petition to the Government right away and ask them to have those mosquitoes
clapped in irons! Kurdish sense!'

Memed Ali flushed and clenched his fists.

'Don't mock me, Agha. I tell you I not give you my cotton.
I not have rice-paddy on village land. There's law. There's
government . . .'

Okchuoglu sprang up, but kept a hold on himself.

'Why can't you fellows understand? I tell you this is a
national crop. That law you keep talking about is out of date.
That was before the new Commissioner came. Do you think
the Government, a great big Government, doesn't know
about mosquitoes and malaria? Of course it does. Otherwise
it would have forbidden rice-growing.'

'We understand very well,' said a villager, 'but we can't
live for six whole months in mud and swamp. We understand all about this national crop, but where are we to go?'

'Tomorrow my men will come and measure your fields.
They'll give you a paper with which you'll get your money

from my office. A whole crop's value without doing a stroke
of work! What more do you want? Mud! What's a little
mud? Were you all born in palaces?'

'But our homes . . . Swamped . . . The children . . .'

Okchuoglu boiled over at last.

'Ungrateful wretches!' he shouted. 'Osman Agha! Tell
them to bring my horse at once. A handful of Kurds who
can't even speak Turkish come to you parroting "the law,
the law" . . . As though their fathers had made this law!
As though they were born with it, the swine!' He strode up
and down, wiping the sweat from his brow. 'And to think
I've always treated you like a father! Two sacks of rice I've
always given each of you at the end of the harvest. Had you
ever seen rice before, you dumb fools? You came to the
Chukurova with nothing but goatskins on your back. Skins,
that's all you ever wore! Now you've come out of your caves
and live in houses like human beings. What more do you
want, ungrateful devils?'

The villagers were petrified. They held their breath.
Okchuoglu's deep voice went booming through the village.
'I'll show you! As sure as my name's Okchuoglu, I'll show
you!' He jumped on his horse. 'Just wait and see what I'll
do to you all!'

He galloped out of the village, raising a cloud of dust. The
villagers stared after him, stiff as stones.

IV

Resul Efendi was lying on the sofa, while his wife sat sewing
near him. A pressure lantern hung from the ceiling, hissing
as it burned.

'Hanum,' said Resul Efendi hesitantly. She raised her

head from her sewing for a moment. 'You say I shouldn't get mixed up in this, but I can't stand it any longer. If you only knew what a fine young man this Commissioner is! He doesn't even know what evil is. That's what tripped him into their nets. If he only learnt the truth about those Aghas, why, by God, he'd blast them all to high heaven.' He licked his lips. 'If I could give him just a little hint ... The doctor would like to, I know, but he doesn't dare. If he'd only troubled to read the Rice Law ... When I hear the things people are saying about him, it brings tears to my eyes.'

'You're always ready to cry for anyone,' said his wife. Resul Efendi could tell she was angry by the way her hands had begun to tremble. 'You'd break your heart for any stranger! Why did he go to those night-clubs? Why did he sign anything that was brought to him? Hatche Hanum's told me he's always dancing attendance on those rice-planters, pandering to their every wish. And who wouldn't? There he is, lording it in Long Rahmet's beautiful house, sleeping on mattresses of down ...'

'Don't say that, Hanum,' cried Resul Efendi. 'He's so young he doesn't know what wickedness is. Somebody should twitch his ears, that's all. Ah, just let me drop him a hint, and just watch!'

'And I'm telling you, Resul Efendi, not to go poking your nose into this business. Everyone would guess it came from you, and then where would we be? All those rice-planters will be after you again like the plague. I beg you, keep out of this and don't go asking for trouble!'

They had been arguing like this for days now, poor Resul Efendi blowing hot and cold with misgiving. He had told himself time and again that the first thing he would do in the morning would be to speak to the Commissioner and make him read the rice-growing regulations, of which he had been carrying a crumpled copy in his pocket for the past week. But in the morning, at the office, the matter would appear in a different light. Visions would arise of the Commissioner set against the rice-planters in a bitter fight and himself Deputy Commissioner again, and he would shudder at the thought. But the worm kept gnawing at him.

That morning, he rose early as usual and went straight to Tewfik's coffee-house. He had fallen into the habit of stopping there for a glass of tea and listening to the town gossip before going on to his office. It was market day and the wares had been set up right in front of the coffee-house. The street was teeming with ragged, barefooted villagers come to sell and buy.

Sergeant Haji Ali, an old friend of Resul Efendi's, greeted him with roars of laughter.

'Eh, Resul, that little whippersnapper of yours! What a man he's turned out to be! How he's fleecing those rice-planters! A hundred thousand liras he's bagged for the permits. Signed five hundred of them in one day, the little rogue! And you wouldn't sign even one of them . . .'

Resul Efendi could contain himself no longer.

'That's sheer slander,' he burst out, flinging caution to the winds. 'He's clean and innocent as on the day he was born.'

The coffee-house hooted with laughter.

'Lay him back in the cradle,' cried Sergeant Haji Ali, 'and see if he doesn't accept bribes even there. Why, he learnt the art in his mother's womb, that one! Otherwise, how could he be such an expert?'

Resul Efendi stalked out of the coffee-house, muttering angrily.

There was nobody in the office. He paced up and down his room, still muttering to himself.

'Today,' he kept saying until his mouth was dry. 'I must speak to him today. Even if they kill me . . . But he won't tell and who will know I did it? They'll never find out . . .'

The Commissioner always arrived on the dot of nine. Resul Efendi recognized his footsteps as he came running up the stairs like a schoolboy and his heart began to pound. He felt suddenly hot all over. With trembling hands he buttoned up his coat, smoothed down his clothes and pulled the crumpled copy of the law out of his pocket.

The Commissioner was at his desk, reading some papers. He looked up with a smile.

'How are things going, Resul Efendi?'

Resul Efendi took a few steps, then stopped. The room had suddenly gone dark about him.

'What's the matter, Resul Efendi?' asked the Commissioner, alarmed. 'Are you sick?'

Weakly Resul Efendi held out the copy of the law. The Commissioner took it and glanced at the title.

'Do sit down, Resul Efendi. Thank you for this.'

Resul Efendi sank into a chair.

'There's something I have to tell you,' he began haltingly. 'Yes, Beyefendi, I have to! You should know how things really stand. But please, I implore you never say Resul told you. The Aghas would skin me alive. Yes, they would, Beyefendi. Don't ever mention my name. Act as though I'm your enemy. You see, I've got a wife and child. A home . . . Never say you heard it from me.'

'Of course I won't,' said the Commissioner, intrigued. 'But what is it?'

'I'm your enemy,' insisted Resul Efendi. 'I've got my knife into you. Don't ever forget that.'

'I won't, Resul Efendi. I understand. Now tell me.'

'Well, Beyefendi . . .' He clasped his hands between his

legs as though trying to hide them. 'It's gossip of course . . .
But people are saying the most impossible things about
you . . .'

The Commissioner's eyes widened.

'What kind of things?' he asked apprehensively.

'Beyefendi, it's all lies . . . Slander, every single word of
it. People are saying you've taken bribes . . . The town's
been talking about nothing else for days. Just malicious
slander . . .'

The Commissioner leapt to his feet.

'It can't be possible! People can't believe such a thing!'

Resul Efendi smiled bitterly.

'No one would have signed those permits as easily as you
did for less than a hundred thousand liras. If you just read
the law, you'll understand.'

'The law?'

'Yes, the rice-growing regulations.'

'But the Agricultural Technician explained everything . . .'

'Beyefendi, he's the rice-planters' man. He has a financial
share in all the rice-fields here.'

The Commissioner had been nagged lately by a feeling that
something fishy was afoot. The doctor for one had seemed
to want to warn him . . . He gave orders that no one should
be admitted and set about reading the law. An hour later
he was through.

'The scoundrels! The crooks!' He went round and round
the room blindly, twisting his long hair and biting his cheeks.
'The ground should be ploughed twice. Not the slightest
hollow in the fields. They must be absolutely level. The
irrigation channels are to be of cement. The Rice Commission
must go and inspect each field before issuing the permit . . .
Partial irrigation . . . Continuous irrigation . . . Unless

these conditions are fulfilled . . . Oh God, what of the permits I've issued?'

He did not know. It had all happened so quickly. His
eyes filled with tears of helplessness. He laid his head on the
table and remained quite still for a while. Then he pressed
the bell for the office boy.

'Fetch Resul Efendi.'

Resul Efendi came in running.

'Take two gendarmes with you. Here's the key to my
house. Have my cases and things brought into this room
here next door. From now on I'm going to sleep right here.'

v

From the foothills of the Taurus mountains, from the upper
reaches of the River Savrun, the Aziz Agha Aqueduct comes
winding swiftly down into the Chukurova plain. Almost as
long as the river itself, this aqueduct is worth a fortune to its
owner for when in the hot summer months the river ebbs
low and the crops risk drying up, the planter who has rented
the Aziz Agha Aqueduct can sit back without a care in the
world and watch the others fly at each other's throats over a
drop of water. However much the level may fall, there is still
enough to irrigate at least two thousand five hundred acres.
The planter's aim is to flood as much land as possible, and
he is blind to villages, houses and farms. For three years now
it was Okchuoglu who had been renting this aqueduct.
Nothing in the world could have made him give up the four
hundred acres around Sazlidere, which would bring him a
net three hundred thousand liras this year.

He had unlocked the sluices five days ago, the very evening
of his dispute with the villagers, but the water had progressed
slowly, draining into the cracked thirsty earth. It was only

on the sixth night that the flood burst into the village, setting pandemonium loose. Dogs barked, donkeys brayed, horses whinnied and oxen bellowed, while the panicking villagers scurried about in the dark, weltering in mud and water, as they carried their belongings up into the *chardaks*.* Their torchwood had been soaked through and in the summer no one bothered to keep any gas for the lamps. Dursun was the only one who had managed to light a lamp, and at last everyone gathered in front of his house as they waited for the day to dawn. A heavy silence weighed like doom over the village. Memed Ali the Kurd was leaning against a mulberry tree, his head bowed, his arms hanging down lifelessly.

Suddenly, an angry voice rose from among the women who were clustered together away from the men. 'Ah, women, there aren't any men left in this village any more! Even Memed Ali's like a eunuch now. In the old day's he'd have made mincemeat of that Okchuoglu.'

'Mother Zeyno's right,' said another woman. 'The fellow's turned the whole village into a lake and there's no one to stand up to him . . .'

'Ah ' cried Zeyno, 'if there'd been just one real man . . .'

'Just one . . .'

'We wouldn't be like this. Flooded out . . .'

The eastern sky was lighting up now and the mountain tops were growing pale. Soon the few clouds on the horizon were purfled with gold, and sunlight struck the flooded fields that glistened like a mirror. The cotton, the sesame, the vegetables, all the newly green crops were under water. In the crude light of day the village was a sorry sight, as though it had been plunged into a bog and pulled out again.

---

* *Chardak*: a kind of open-air hut built high on piles, roofed and with a ramp about it, where the peasants sleep during the hot summer nights.

Memed Ali had not moved and no one dared to go near him. It was Zeyno who spoke to him first.

'Where's your manhood, Memed Ali?' she cried. 'The village is a lake. We're being kicked out of our homes, kicked out by that dirty swine Okchuoglu. Isn't there a single man left in this village? That's what I'm asking you.'

Memed Ali gave her a bloodshot look. His face had taken on a leaden hue.

'Ah!' he groaned, clenching his fists and straining his whole body as if in pain. 'Ah, Zeyno . . .'

She suddenly felt sorry for him.

'What to do?' he said desperately. 'Tell me, what? Kill Okchuoglu and go to mountain? But Okchuoglu not one man. Many, many Okchuoglus . . . I mixed up. I mad. I burst!'

Zeyno put her hand on his shoulder.

'Well,' she said, 'let's decide what we're going to do. Can we live six months in water? Why, the houses'll collapse in less than a month and we'll all be left in the open!'

'Let's go to the Commissioner,' suggested Dursun.

'He's Okchuoglu's man,' objected someone.

'So what?' expostulated Zeyno. 'What if he were his own father? Anybody who sees us in this state . . .'

'Zeyno right,' said Memed Ali.

There was a long consultation and it was finally decided that the whole village, young and old, would set off for the town right away to see the Commissioner.

Zeyno set about dispensing instructions right and left.

'Now, women, you all lock your doors. And mind you, no changing clothes! You go just as you are, muddy and all. And if you're not muddy enough, squat down in the mud until you are. Give your children a good coating too and carry them along. And if that Commissioner won't listen to us, we'll walk on, just as we are, right up to Ankara. There's a law in this country. There's a government!'

An hour later the whole village set off, led by Zeyno. They waded through the flooded land until at last they came to the main road. The women carried their babies in their arms while the small children clung to their skirts.

The heat of the day was upon them now and they moved stirring up a cloud of dust. By the time they reached the town they had lost all human aspect. Dust had settled over their crust of mud, and their eyebrows and eyelashes were powdered white. It was a startling sight for the townspeople, who were not slow to realize that something was up. Shopkeepers pulled down their shutters with a great clatter, people in the coffee-houses threw away their cards and converged towards the Commissioner's office. Soon the whole town was gathered there.

Zeyno was shouting at the top of her voice.

'Commissioner! Come out, Commissioner, and look at us!' The sight of the swelling crowd spurred her on. 'Look, look, good Moslems! See what Okchuoglu's brought upon us. Is it right to treat fellow-Moslems so? Tell me, is it right? Is it right to flood a huge inhabited village? Look at us! Let the Commissioner look! Perhaps his frozen heart will melt a little . . .'

Dursun and Memed Ali left the crowd with Zeyno still shouting, and went up to the Commissioner.

'Okchuoglu has flooded our village for his rice. All our crops are under water. We're up to our waists in water. You must do something . . .'

The Commissioner stared. 'Okchuoglu's not going to plant rice in the village too, surely?'

'He is. He's released the water and turned the village into a lake.'

'Good heavens!'

The Commissioner went outside. All eyes were levelled accusingly at him. He wanted to say something, to beg their forgiveness for the wretched state they were in, but he could only stand there, a dry lump in his throat.

'What are you staring at us for, son?' shouted Zeyno. 'This is your own handiwork. Fine work too! Giving permits to plant rice in a village! We'd seen everything, but not this yet! You thought up this one, man. Well, how do you like it? So rice is a national crop, eh? So you decide it's to be grown in all the villages and in all the houses as well? Have you no fear of God? Look at us. Don't we belong to this nation too? Look, look! See these poor children? But no, you're Okchuoglu's man! Well, I'm going to show these people to the Commander-in-Chief. I'll put them on the train and take them straight to Ankara, so the Commander-in-Chief can see them. "Here," I'll say, "these are your villagers, these creatures drowned in mud and water! Take them, take them! . . ." '

The Commissioner was struck dumb. He turned back quickly and shut the door behind him. He could still hear Zeyno's voice, a sound like thunder in his ears.

Memed Ali and Dursun were looking at him expectantly.

'Which of you is village headman?' he asked after a while.

'Seyfi Ali is the headman,' answered Dursun. 'But he's Okchuoglu's man. He wouldn't come with us.'

'Tell the villagers to go back. I'm coming over right away.'

He summoned the Agricultural Technician. 'Collect the Rice Commission,' he ordered. 'We're all going to Sazlidere.'

'Ah, sir,' said the other ingratiatingly, 'these planters . . . They're insatiable.'

The jeep could not get through because of the water.

It had to stop two miles from the village. The members of the Commission rolled up their trousers and waded on. The village was deserted. They climbed on to a cart and waited, staring at the water that poured by unceasingly. Streams of yellow liquid were streaming down the dung heaps and the whole place smelled of wet manure.

The rumbling of the crowd returning from the town was gradually growing louder.

VI

This unexpected piling up of events had shaken the Commissioner into a new awareness. He was thin and worn now, but his eyes shone with an unusual brightness. In the space of a few weeks he had grown wise to a lifetime's teaching. He had visited the villages one by one, staying with the peasants and sharing their hardships. Now, every morning before going to the office, he joined the sick queue of villagers who came from all over the district. He talked to them and learnt even more about the lies and shifts, the twists and turns of the rice Aghas. Taking the Rice Commission along, he visited as many as five plantations a day and discovered that not one of them abided by the regulations. He refused to issue the much-awaited permits for both of Murtaza Agha's one thousand five hundred acre paddies when he found that they skirted villages and had no irrigation channels to speak of.

Tewfik Ali Bey, Kemal Tashan, Mustafa Patir and several other planters had also been refused permits and they were growing desperate. If they sowed their rice later than May, the yield would be nowhere near the usual eighty to one, and might even drop to less than forty to one. They decided to tackle the Commissioner gently at first, and the small,

aged, hunchbacked Mufti of the town was chosen to plead
their cause.

'My son,' began the Mufti, 'rice has always been sown this
way. Those regulations are so impractical that they've
never been taken into account. You see, whatever you do
there will always be mosquitoes. This is the Chukurova.
What, no mosquitoes in this heat? Why, rice or not, we've
always had them! You must not be so uncompromising
or . . .'

'What are you talking about?' the Commissioner interrupted him sharply. 'Do you mean . . .?' Suddenly he
pointed to the door. 'You may go! And you needn't come
here again. This is none of your business.'

The dumbfounded Mufti shuffled off hurriedly, muttering
prayers. 'Allah guard us from evil! Allah save us all! This
man isn't a Commissioner, he's a fire-eater. Allah protect
us!'

The rice-planters crowded around him. 'What happened,
Mufti Efendi?'

He closed his eyes and counted his beads. 'Allah protect
us, Allah protect us!'

The rice-planters now decided to call on Riza Degnek.
He was the son of a rich Agha who had left him a farm, half a
dozen houses and as many shops and two inns. It had taken
him only a few years to run through this inheritance, but
even after spending his last penny there had been no apparent
change in his life and habits. His clothes were still the
smartest in town and he had never been seen with an un-
pressed suit. He it was who initiated gambling in the town,
and he still gambled more than anyone else. At ease with
great and small, he always managed to win everybody's
favour. A couple of days were enough for him to become
bosom friends with any newcomer of importance. 'He's got

the devil's charm,' people said of him. Whenever there was a bribe to be offered, Riza Degnek was the man for the job. It never took him more than a week to suborn even the most honourable official.

'There's a good two thousand in this for you,' said the rice-planters.

Riza Degnek smiled. 'Fifteen thousand,' he declared, 'is the least I can take.'

'We'll do everything for you, Riza,' pleaded Murtaza Agha. 'I, for one, will be your slave. Just show yourself, just show what you're capable of and there's nothing you can't ask from us.'

Resul Efendi, however, had warned the Commissioner that he should expect a visit from Riza Degnek any day now. So he was ready when an obsequiously simpering man entered the room with a bow and a scrape.

'Ah your Excellency! I must plead forgiveness for not calling on you before. The daily grind, you know . . . You were busy too. I came once, but your Excellency was out inspecting the paddies. Please excuse me. To fail in courtesy towards a man like you! It's unforgivable . . .'

The Commissioner looked at him coldly. 'What do you want?'

'Only to pay my . . .'

'The real reason,' shouted the Commissioner. 'Come to the point!'

'But, Beyefendi, I called . . . The reason . . .'

The Commissioner pointed to the door.

'Get out! At once!'

Riza Degnek found himself walking down the stairs in a daze.

'I'll be damned!' he muttered. 'The bastard kicked us out well and truly . . .' Suddenly he laughed. 'Those rice lords are going to have trouble with this lad. He'll make them sweat. Kicked me out. Me! Kicked out!'

He was still smiling when he entered the town club. The rice-planters took this for a sign of victory and pressed around him to shake his hand.

'How did you manage it?'

'Nothing doing,' chuckled Riza Degnek. 'Never came across the likes of him before. As hard as flint. Nothing doing with him.'

The rice-planters were astounded. How could it have come to this? Their whole fortune at the mercy of a mere boy! Their rage knew no bounds. Murtaza Agha decided it was high time for radical measures. One night he hired men to stone the Commissioner's windows. Another night he had shots fired into his room. Then the official jeep was tampered with and the Commissioner had to set out for the rice-fields on horseback. The restaurant owner was bribed to send him spoiled food. He fined him and made do with bread and cheese for a while.

An average of fifty telegrams a day denouncing the Commissioner were dispatched to Ankara. The town's letter-writer, Politician Ahmet, was entrusted with this task, for long years of experience had made him a master in the art of making up criminal records for commissioners. The first day's batch of telegrams were signed by the rice-planters, the second day's by the village headmen, of which there were sixty in the district, the third day's by the mayor and the political party leaders. Then came the turn of the villagers. Twenty-five signed for Chinar village, seventy for Chiyanli, more for Chaygechit, Aliler, Oksuzler . . . Long lists of names . . . The telegrams were addressed to the County Governor, to the Prime Minister, to the President of the Republic, to the Ministry of the Interior, to the Ministry of

Agriculture, even to the Ministry of Education. Every evening the Postmaster would bring copies of the telegrams to the Commissioner, who after the first shock when he had almost wept with impotent rage was now taking the matter in his stride. Resul Efendi had hastened to inform him that such telegrams were nothing new. Politician Ahmet had been plying this thriving trade for the past twenty-five years. His job was to fabricate brand-new offences for troublesome commissioners. Still, the charges against Fikret Irmakli would have made anyone's hair stand on end.

'Blood drips from my pen,' Politician Ahmet boasted proudly.

But all these telegrams were of no avail. The Commissioner remained in his post. He was not even reprimanded.

Time was running out. Champing the bit, the rice-planters paced the market-place, pouring out their woes to whoever would listen.

'How can he do this? He's only a chit of a boy who doesn't know what he's letting himself in for.'

'He seemed so tractable, so well-bred! To think that all this time he was nurturing forty vipers in his breast . . .'

'He's mad . . . Mad! Someone should make him understand the importance of rice for this country. If only he realized rice doesn't cause malaria . . .'

'Who ever heard of rice causing malaria?'

'Why, we've had malaria here since time out of mind!'

Then, one Wednesday night, the rice-planters conferred till morning. Finally they came to a decision. All the fields were to be planted the very next day and let the Commissioner do his worst. He certainly could not hang them! In addition, a five-man mission would set off for Ankara right away to lobby for the Commissioner's removal.

Early on Thursday morning the sluices were opened. The

news that the water had been released without authorization burst on the town like a bomb. Nothing like this had ever happened before.

VII

The Commissioner was now deep in the struggle. With the help of Blind Jemal and Pehlivan Usta, he launched an intensive campaign against rice-growing. Blind Jemal earned his living as a letter-writer. 'It's rice that killed my brother,' he would claim. 'Without all those rice-paddies, there'd never have been malaria . . .' Groups of villagers would throng into the town with heart-rending stories about the ravages of the fever. The headman of Tartarli assembled some forty splenetic children from his village, with swollen bellies, spindly legs, scrawny faces and enormous eyes, and herded them into the Commissioner's presence. The Commissioner had photographs taken which he forwarded to the Ministry of Health.

Then one night the rice-planters tried to have Blind Jemal shot, but he escaped with a short bout in hospital. His assailants were never discovered. And one morning Pehlivan Usta awoke to find his orange grove levelled to the ground, with all the trees systematically hacked down. Other attacks of the kind slowed down the campaign. Only one or two of the village headmen held firm.

Resul Efendi was afraid. He denounced the Commissioner to all and sundry, in the street, in the coffee-house, and sometimes even at home to his wife. He knew that if the rice-planters ever got wind of the part he had played, it would be the end of him.

'Ah, my friends, I keep telling him, "Don't do this, my son. You can't fight the planters. Even the Government

yields the palm to them." But no! He will not listen. He
just won't! What a quiet, pleasant young man he seemed
when he first came here! I simply can't make out what
possessed him all of a sudden. He's deaf to all advice. If
you ask me, it's the shock of seeing all those villagers from
Sazlidere marching up to him covered in mud. That made
him go off his head . . .'

Such talk led the rice-planters to believe that Resul Efendi
was their man, and they confided in him unreservedly.
Okchuoglu even tried to make use of him.

'You must explain to that Commissioner,' he urged, 'that
I'm not among those intriguing against him. Tell him to
stop harrying me. It'll do him no good to gang up with the
likes of that Kurdish bandit.'

The Commissioner had placed a guard of seven gendarmes
at his sluices, and his newly sown fields were in danger of
draining dry before the rice had even sprouted. However, it
did not take him long to bribe the gendarmes and the water
was released again. Memed Ali informed the Commissioner
of this. The gendarmes were replaced, but the new ones
lasted only a couple of days.

'Commissioner,' begged Memed Ali, 'I keep village dry.
I watch over Okchuoglu's water. Please, please let me . . .
Our right, since flood in our village! Our right . . .'

'Not yet, Memed Ali,' the Commissioner would put him
off. 'I've reported the situation to the Gendarme Commander. We must wait.'

The sluice gates to the other rice-paddies were under the
stone bridge on the edge of the town. Ten gendarmes had
been stationed there. At any hour of the day or the night,
the Commissioner would leave whatever he was doing
and rush off to see that the gendarmes were doing their
job.

'That Commissioner's thirsting for trouble!'

'And he'll find it, mark my words.'

'He'll get himself shot down like a dog.'

Resul Efendi was terrified. He knew the incensed rice-planters would have no qualms in doing away with the Commissioner one dark night, and no one any the wiser.

'It's not that I care,' he would be careful to repeat publicly, 'but if he's killed this town's going to get a bad name. We'll all be disgraced, my friends. "Fikret Bey, my son," I say to him, "what do you think you're doing, roaming about like this in the dead of night? Are you a gendarme?" He just turns a deaf ear . . .'

It was getting on for midnight. The murmur of the Savrun river filled the earth-scented night air. The Commissioner walked towards the sluice gates and the gleaming pebbles of the river bed crunched under his steps. The starlight was reflected in the dark flowing water and the bridge stood out white against the tenuous darkness of the night. No sound came from the sleeping town, except the whistle of the night watchman and the untimely crowing of a cock. He was thinking of the Sultan Ahmet Park in Istanbul and the Square at Beyazit with its fountain. The trams, the buses, the cars . . . And again and always before his eyes the Beyazit fountain and the students hurrying out of the University near by to get a place on the benches around it. What was he doing here? Was it worth all this fuss? Then he called to mind Zeyno and Memed Ali the Kurd. 'Yes, it's worth it. Just for an old bandit, for Mother Zeyno and for those wide-eyed children. It's worth fighting for. It's even worth dying for . . .' He realized he was gripping the butt of his pistol with all his strength. It seemed strange to be holding a pistol. 'It's worth it ' he repeated. 'It's worth it, but how will it all end? I know I'm right. I've got the law with me.

But all those complaints to Ankara . . . Will they influence the Ministry to do something against me? Ah, never mind! I wish Nermin were with me now. How proud she'd be to see me fighting this web of intrigue all alone! No, not quite alone. I've got Resul Efendi on my side. He knows them all through and through. How he hates them! How he fears them too . . . And I? Fear? Maybe . . .'

Suddenly a shadow appeared behind the scrub. An ambush? In a flash he had flung himself down.

'Don't move or I fire!' he shouted.

'Commissioner,' came a whining voice out of the darkness. 'It's only Murtaza.'

The Commissioner rose.

'Let me kiss your hands and feet, my Commissioner,' began Murtaza Agha. 'Don't do this to me. I've put all my capital into this crop and it's drying up. Have some pity! If I go bankrupt at my age, I'll be the laughing-stock of the whole town.'

They came to the night post. One of the gendarmes was keeping vigil. The water channels were quite dry.

'Say something, Commissioner! Don't kill me. I'll die of grief, and so will my family. My two boys are at a university like the one you went to, and I must see them through . . .'

He was still pleading as they came back through the deserted market-place.

'Say something, Commissioner! I'll never plant rice again, never! Not this way . . . Why don't you say something?'

They were before the Commissioner's office now. Without a word, the Commissioner started up the steps.

'Do as you like, then,' shouted Murtaza Agha after him. 'But you'd better think twice. You're a young man. It will be a pity . . .'

The door was slammed vigorously in his face.

That very night, Murtaza Agha, Mustafa Patir and two others set out for Ankara by car.

Alone among the rice-planters Okchuoglu had managed to attain his end by bribing the gendarmes. He swaggered proudly up and down the market-place switching his boots with his silver-topped whip.

'So the Commissioner ordered our rice-paddies to be dried up, did he?' he sneered. 'How clever of him! So he planted gendarmes at our sluice gates, eh? A brainwave! And the villagers of Sazlidere had to complain about the mud, eh? Well, now I've loosed such a flood of water on them that they're up to their waists in it. Let them see what mud really is! I'll bring their houses down over their heads.'

At last, driven to despair, Memed Ali and Zeyno appealed to the Commissioner for the last time.

'Water wrecking our houses,' said Memed Ali. 'Commissioner, please give permission we do something . . .'

'We're living in water,' cried Zeyno, beside herself. 'Fields, cotton, houses, all swamped. All the children are sick by now. You must do something quickly.'

'I've telephoned the County Seat for new gendarmes,' replied the Commissioner, bowing his head miserably. 'What else can I do?'

Zeyno grasped Memed Ali by the arm.

'Come,' she said angrily. 'We'll deal with this ourselves.'

VIII

In most villages of the Chukurova plain the huts are built of brushwood, but the Sazlidere peasants use reeds for their walls and plaster them with mud. The roofs are of thin rushes, packed tight layer upon layer, and as impervious to rain as sheet-iron. But now the wet reed walls had begun to sag under the weight of the roof. And still the waters went pouring through the village. Okchuoglu had kept his word . . .

'That Okchuoglu,' declared Zeyno. 'I'll show him, as sure as my name's Zeyno. He'll see who's stronger, the master or the people!'

Zeyno was over fifty. She had a round face with a small pointed chin and bright cheerful black eyes under delicate eyebrows. Long ago her husband had gone off to the wars and never returned, and she had lived on the produce of the thirty acres he had left her. It was plenty for her and she had even been able to adopt three orphans and marry them off. The whole village looked upon her as a mother, for she was always ready to help anyone in need. Only she could break up fights and patch up enmities. But she had a temper, and when it flared up she would shout and swear like a man. 'Mother Zeyno's turned wildcat again,' the villagers would say, carefully keeping out of her way.

After the flooding of the village, she had gone from house to house, caring for the sick and trying to cheer up the dejected villagers. 'How are Okchuoglu's ducklings?' she would joke as she looked in at the door of each hut. But for the past two days she had not opened her mouth. Her long skirts tucked up, she waded about the village, her face sullen and her eyes screwed up. The villagers watched her warily as again and again she planted herself under Memed Ali's *chardak*, glaring up angrily.

Since their last appeal to the Commissioner, it seemed as though Memed Ali had washed his hands of the whole business. He had retired into his *chardak*, and there he lay all day long singing a bitter, melancholy song that never ended. On and on he sang without a break, and as he sang one could see a lonely flock of cranes flying high and far in

the distant skies. From time to time he would heave a deep
sigh that somehow was part of the sad song, and those who
heard him wanted to sob their hearts out.

It was late afternoon and the dark shadows of the hills
were lengthening towards the east when Zeyno suddenly
burst out of her house and went splashing her way to Memed
Ali's *chardak*.

'Come right down, Memed Ali, and stop that moaning.
Wailing like an old woman from morning to night! The
whole village is like a funeral, thanks to you!'

Her angry voice rang out over the village. Memed Ali
stopped singing for a moment, then started again. Zeyno
was infuriated.

'Coward!' she screamed. 'Eunuch! Have you lost your
manhood too like the rest of the village?'

At last he clambered down slowly, with a dull, bemused
air as though walking in his sleep.

'Those worms who call themselves men,' cried Zeyno,
'are sitting in the shadow of Dursun's hut and they're thinking. Thinking! May their heads drop off! Come . . .'

She led the way to Dursun's hut where the men were
hanging about, downcast and idle.

'Eh, Okchuoglu's women,' she taunted them, 'here's
Memed Ali. He's going to sit with you and think too, while
the water destroys the village!'

'There's a government and there are gendarmes . . .'
murmured one or two men, their eyes fixed on the ground.
'What is there we can do?'

Zeyno plumped her hands on her hips.

'I spit on you, shameless cowards! So there's nothing you
can do, eh? The gendarmes have been bribed. All right,
but what about you? Can't you guard the water? Isn't the
law with us?'

Everyone in the village had rushed up at the sound of Zeyno's shouting. There was a stirring and a muttering among the men.

'That scoundrel's flouting the law,' continued Zeyno. 'The Commissioner's done his best even though he's only a chit of a boy. It's up to us now. Let's break down the sluice gate and keep watch ourselves.'

'Zeyno right!' shouted Memed Ali suddenly. 'I go!'

Zeyno turned to the women.

'Come on. Get some picks and shovels. These creatures can guard the water in the village!'

'Come on! Quick!'

The crowd of women broke up and made for the huts. In a flash they were back again, carrying picks and shovels.

Suddenly the men rose.

'Get a move on!' someone shouted.

Zeyno led the march at a run. The women followed her and behind them came the men. Only the old people remained in the village. The rumbling crowd reached the dike on Sulemish hill just as the sun was setting. It was Zeyno who struck the first blow at the sluice gate before the eyes of the dumbfounded gendarmes.

'Smash it down!'

In a trice the sluices were breached and the muddy waters were gushing forth noisily towards the River Savrun.

'Block it here!'

Soon the channel leading to the rice-fields was dammed up, while the gendarmes still stood by gaping.

'Well, my lads?' Zeyno laughed in their faces. 'So you thought you were here to guard Okchuoglu's sluice gate, eh? Poor little lambs!'

'Thirty of us'll stand guard here,' said Dursun. 'The

women are to go to the village and bring food and guns. Okchuoglu's men won't be long coming . . .'

'You not mind Okchuoglu!' cried Memed Ali, brandishing a rifle. 'He come with thousand men, a whole tribe, but they never get near water. No one get near. Not while Memed Ali alive.'

Okchuoglu was blind with rage at the news. Pistol in hand, he jumped on his horse and headed for the dike, murder in his heart.

'What are we coming to?' he kept repeating to himself. 'That a handful of barefooted peasants should dare wreck my dike! I must kill them, every one of them . . .'

At Narlibahche, he cooled off and reined in, forcing himself to think more calmly. Then he turned the horse towards Sazlidere.

He burst into the village at full speed and galloped straight up to the headman's house. The water had drained away and the village was drier now. The women and children hurried out of their huts to watch him. They were laughing in their sleeves.

'Just you wait,' Okchuoglu growled. 'I'll get even with you some time.'

The headman was at his door, looking tired and dejected.

'Seyfi Ali,' said Okchuoglu, 'call up the villagers. I'm giving three hundred liras for each house. And two hundred liras per acre of cotton. But everyone's to keep away from this village until the autumn. And I'll pay for the houses that have collapsed too.'

'Now you're talking, Agha!' said the headman with relief. 'That's the spirit! Who'll want to stay in the village now? They'll all go.'

Okchuoglu waited while word was sent to the men on guard at the dike. He repeated his offer. Nobody said a word. He took out his wallet and began handing out the money.

'This is for the houses,' he said. 'Come tomorrow and get your money for the crops. No one's to stay in the village. Clear?'

A few dissenting murmurs were quickly silenced.

'Keep quiet, you fools! Okchuoglu's sure to get the better of the Commissioner in the end and we'll find ourselves flooded again. This is a lot of money.'

Memed Ali never stirred, but nobody noticed that he had not taken any money. As for Zeyno, she was struck dumb at the sudden turn of events.

Okchuoglu mounted his horse with a huge grin on his face. Next he went to the letter-writer. As soon as Politician Ahmet saw his smirk, he grasped the situation.

'You know what to write,' Okchuoglu laughed.

'Five hundred thousand?' asked Politician Ahmet.

'Why not?'

'To the High Authority of the Rice Commission,' ran the petition. 'The Rice Commission have cut off the water from my rice-fields and caused me damages amounting to five hundred thousand liras, on the ground that there is a village in the middle of them. This is a deliberate fabrication on the part of my enemies and certain members of the Rice Commission. As early as last March, when the rice-sowing plans were being drawn up, the village of Sazlidere was purchased together with all its houses, and for three months now no living creature has set foot in it. I require that this should be ascertained by an immediate survey and request that water be released on to my fields without delay. I also inform the Commission that I am taking legal action to recover the losses I have sustained to date.'

When the Rice Commission went to Sazlidere the next

afternoon, they found the village deserted and echoing with emptiness. While they stood staring in silence at the desolate scene, a figure appeared in the distance and came walking towards them. It was Memed Ali. His face was yellow and his arms hung down lifelessly.

'What's all this, Memed Ali?' asked the Commissioner. 'Where's everyone?'

Memed Ali smiled grimly.

'Okchuoglu bought houses, crops. Men left.'

'What are you doing here then?' asked Kemal Tashan.

'This my village! My right . . . I not take Okchuoglu's money, not I! I die but not leave. I stay here with wife and children. I go on living right here. This village not empty.'

Since the village was still inhabited there was nothing the Rice Commission could do but reject Okchuoglu's petition.

'Swine!' raved Okchuoglu. 'They're all against me. As for that Kurd . . . I'll teach him. I'll have him killed and buried in the middle of my land!'

He had his men for tackling such problems.

'Deal with the fellow straight away,' he ordered. 'I want him done away with. Wounded at the very least . . .'

Memed Ali had been expecting some kind of reprisal. That night he lay in wait in the shadow of his *chardak*, his rifle on his lap.

'If only Okchuoglu come himself . . . I settle his account right now. Ah, if only . . . Yes, I shoot him right between the eyes!'

It was past midnight when he sighted the five figures.

'Who's that?' he called out, his finger on the trigger.

The answer was a volley of shots. The old bandit riposted instantly. With the speed of a machine-gun, his rifle raked the darkness before him. His attackers had flung themselves on the ground at the first shot and soon there was no sign of them.

The next morning Okchuoglu rode into the village bringing along a relative of Memed Ali's from the town, the shopkeeper Reshid Agha.

'Why are you staying,' shouted Okchuoglu. 'What good will it do you? The whole village has gone. I'll give you a thousand liras. I'll give you whatever you want, but leave now. What can you gain by ruining me?'

Reshid Agha took Memed Ali aside and talked to him persistently for over an hour. Memed Ali did not once open his mouth, while the two others talked themselves hoarse till evening.

It was not so easy for Okchuoglu to by-pass the law this time. New gendarmes had been posted who would not be bribed. Unless something was done quickly, Okchuoglu would have no rice crop to speak of.

IX

The rice-planters had never encountered such a hard nut to crack. Civil servants, however intractable, had always been dealt with one way or another. But this chit of a Commissioner had defeated them all. There was nothing for it but to wait and hope that the delegation they had sent to Ankara would have more luck.

The villagers were pleased. With many of the fields planted to half their capacity and most of them only partially irrigated, they were less plagued by mosquitoes this year. Some villages were even quite rid of them.

Another unheard-of change had occurred. The villagers were now admitted directly into the presence of the Commissioner whenever they wished. Up to that time, the Com-

missioner's office had been like another town club where the
notables chose to pass the time of the day. A common peasant
could never have his business seen to unless he obtained
proper backing from one of the rich landowners, who as a
result wielded unchallenged power in the villages. Their
whole prestige was at stake now.

'A scandal!' was the angry comment. 'The Government's
representative receiving barefooted, unkempt peasants and
chatting away with them all day long! It just goes to show
this isn't a job for children. A boy only yesterday out of
school, and here he is a Commissioner! Do they think it's
so easy? Here's the living proof of it. A fine mess of things
he's made since he arrived here!'

'He's turned the Government building into a coffee-house
for peasants!'

'Times have changed indeed! That a Commissioner should
take a stand against the notables of the town, that he should
compromise the whole rice crop of the area and then spring
to attention when that mere peasant Osman, from Vayvayli
village, enters his office!'

'Well, he won't be here long now. They won't come back
empty-handed from Ankara.'

'They never have.'

'He'll soon be transferred.'

'Yes, he'll come to his senses in some God-forsaken
frontier province.'

Osman from Vayvayli village was a small man of about
sixty with a cheerful face and white beard. He owned
twenty-five acres of land which, in spite of his age, he har-
vested all by himself. He was in the habit of dressing up
when he went to town, and anyone would have taken him
for a retired civil servant. He even carried a walking-stick.
This enraged the Aghas.

'A mere peasant,' they sniffed, 'and just look at him! A man should know his place . . .'

Osman took no notice of them. But in the village he would don his old shalvar-trousers and set himself to the plough, dusty and barefooted, his cracked feet splaying out on the earth.

Osman had soon become great friends with the Commissioner, to whom he had been introduced by Resul Efendi. He would call on him often, staying for at least an hour, being a talkative man.

That morning it was half past nine when Osman entered the Commissioner's office.

'Why, Osman Agha, how are you?' exclaimed the Commissioner with pleasure. 'You haven't been to see me for ages.'

'Ah, Commissioner, I just couldn't come. No, I really couldn't . . .'

'But why?'

'Well, it's like this. I like you and I come to visit you. But those rice-planters are trying to use me. They won't leave me in peace. "Tell the Commissioner to give up," they keep harping at me. "Anyway," they say, "this is bound to end badly for him." So you see . . . I thought I'd better not come to you again. But then I said, I've done nothing wrong. On the contrary, I'll warn my Commissioner against these monsters. I'll tell my brave lad . . .'

The Commissioner laughed. Then Osman started to talk as usual.

'Seven children I've given to this ack earth, all of malaria. Just because those Aghas had to grow rice I have sat at a blind hearth these many years. So how can I come and say: "Take their money, Commissioner, or they'll kill you! Flood the land and let the mosquitoes take over!" You should see those mosquitoes, Commissioner, when they start whirling like storm-clouds in the sky! There's no escaping them even under nets. They slash through them and devour you. All through the summer, there's no sleep for us, no rest till dawn. No rest for the horses and cattle either. Their backs are all torn and bloody in the morning . . .'

The Commissioner listened, thinking all the while of the children brought in carts, shaking with fever, their eyes overrun by flies, their necks and faces red with mosquito bites, and of the women lying against the surgery walls with sunken eyes.

'How can it be? How, how? How can the Government sit back and watch such a tragedy,' he said. 'Just so that a few landowners should make easy profits . . . How, how can it be possible?'

And then one morning the delegation returned from Ankara. One after the other the shining cars drove slowly through the town. The rice-planters were leaning out of the car windows and greeting the shopkeepers exultantly. They stopped at the market-place, which in a minute was thronged with the triumphant travellers, their relatives, the aqueduct owners, the hangers-on and all those who made a living from rice-growing.

Murtaza Agha began to blow his horn in the midst of the crowd.

'I went to the Minister of the Interior and said: "Efendi, it isn't a Commissioner you've sent us, it's a feudal lord! We can't tolerate such a thing in this country any longer. Thanks to our Republican Government, thanks to our great leaders, the days of feudal despots are long over. We've raised our country to the level of Europe now. I'm only a peasant," I said, "a farmer, and yet for the sake of this fatherland I've put all I have into the land. And then, here

comes this relic of a feudal lord, blustering around, cutting
off our water, using the nation's gendarmes for his own cruel
aims! If it weren't for our country," I said, "if it weren't
for our heroic army, I wouldn't sow a single grain of rice.
No, Efendi! I'd plant cotton instead. This is a free country
now, so how is it you send us this tyrant who takes bribes
and bleeds the people white?" And then I said: "Long live
our Party!" That's what I said, and at that he sat up and
looked thoughtfully at me. He scratched his bald head.
"All right, Murtaza Bey," he said. "I get your point. I'll
deal with the man." "Thank you, Pasha," I said. "You're
safeguarding my family and the food of our army from
oppression," I said. And now, my friends, Murtaza Agha's
going to give him such a send-off the whole of the Chukurova
will stand agape. But what's the good?' he broke off, suddenly
tearful. 'He's ruined me. My rice will hardly yield ten to
one this year. I'm going to lose and lose . . .'

The news was a staggering blow for Resul Efendi. He
remained riveted to his chair, staring in front of him, all
the blood drained from his face, and it was only towards noon
that he was able to pull himself together.

'I'm finished,' he moaned. 'I'm dead, Commissioner . . .
To think I had only a year to go for my pension. Ah,
Fikret Bey, if only you'd been a little more careful. Just a
little handling, and this wouldn't have happened. Ah
youth! . . .'

'What is it, Resul Efendi?' asked the Commissioner
anxiously.

'You've been transferred.'

'How do you know? Has an order come?'

'No, not yet. But the rice-planters have come back and
they're celebrating.'

'Well, what of it?'

'They wouldn't celebrate for nothing, not them. You've been transferred. And I . . . Ah, only one year!'

This can't be! thought the Commissioner, holding his head in his hands. Suddenly, the world was huge and desolate and he was sinking into a horrible darkness. He felt a tangible loneliness, sharp as a knife, piercing him to the very marrow of his bones. He worked on until evening, unconscious of who came and went, of what he signed and what he said. A pain was spreading within him which he could not locate, but it was there. He felt it. Could it be fear? What was he afraid of? The worst that could happen to him was to be transferred. What was it, then? He was just afraid, unaccountably afraid. That night he lay huddled in his bed, sleepless, his heart beating. Once he rose, loaded his pistol and put it under his pillow, but the smell of greasing oil was strange and disturbing to him.

He dressed early and walked down to the banks of the Savrun. The river was an amber yellow. He reflected bitterly that the whole town drank of this murky water polluted by the outflow from the rice-paddies higher up. It was a still, oppressive morning and soon the sun would be striking down, heavy as lead. Again, a sudden unreasonable fear seized him. He turned and almost ran back to his office, where he ordered tea and ate a roll of bread.

Towards eleven o'clock Resul Efendi burst into the room with a sheaf of jumbled papers in his hands.

'Didn't I say so?' he said weakly, holding out the papers tremulously.

The Commissioner read them through twice.

'So it's true . . . So it's the eastern wastes for me now. Commissioner of Kagizman in the Province of Kars . . . They certainly don't grow rice there on the frontier! Well, Resul Efendi, I see they've made you Deputy Commissioner again. It seems as if you'll have to sign all those permits after all . . .'

Resul Efendi smiled.

'But they won't make any profit this year. It's a day after the fair . . . They won't even cover their expenses. The planting season's over! Serve them right! Let them plant away now!'

'So this great big plain will be a marsh half of the year . . . People will go on dying of malaria so that one or two men should make easy money . . . And we, watching it all, helpless . . . Resul Efendi, you must arrange for my transport tomorrow. Find me a car.'

'They'll never give you a car . . .'

'Something else, then. A horse, a donkey, a cart. It doesn't matter what, but I want to leave early tomorrow morning.'

Resul Efendi's face was screwed up in thought.

'Wait, Commissioner, I know. Uncle Hamza's the only one who'll dare take you. He's got an old Ford, a 1917 model, but with some luck it might get to the station without breaking down.'

'Good. And do you know what I'll do, Resul Efendi? I'll go straight to Ankara, to the Ministry and tell them what I've seen with my own eyes. I won't give up the fight.'

Resul Efendi smiled wistfully.

'Fight . . .' he murmured.

'That's right, Resul Efendi. I'll fight to the bitter end.'

On the following morning a few curious townspeople and some peasants had gathered outside the Government building. It was a hot, stifling day. The servants were loading the Commissioner's suitcases and his camp bed into a dilapidated heap of rusty iron that throbbed away obstreperously. A single headlamp dangled from the end of a wire in front, and the remains of a hood flopped dismally all about it.

The Commissioner shook hands with Resul Efendi and the few officials who had come to see him off. Then he climbed in beside old Uncle Hamza. The car jerked off with a loud explosion of the engine.

In the market-place the shopkeepers were at their doorways, staring. The rice-planters had gathered in Tewfik's coffee-house and they all roared with glee as the Commissioner went by.

'There he goes, the apple of my eye, our Commissioner!' shouted Murtaza Agha.

The Commissioner stared straight ahead, steeling himself against the jeering group. But when they came to the bridge, a huge crowd was waiting for them. Knowing what was coming, Uncle Hamza accelerated, but the crowd closed in and an ear-splitting clanging broke out. The Commissioner started up fearfully and saw what seemed to him an army of small boys, each one holding a tin can and drumming on it with all his might.

In Tewfik's coffee-house, Murtaza Agha heard the din.

'There he goes, the apple of my eye!' he gloated. 'See what a send-off I'm giving him? A hundred and fifty cans! As good as Allah's thunder!'

The car had disentangled itself from the crowd and the bridge was now far behind, but the drumming still rang in the Commissioner's ears.

'What were they beating those cans for?' he asked at last.

'It's the send-off,' explained Uncle Hamza. 'The Aghas always do that for Government officials forced to go like you . . .'

The Commissioner bowed his head and a bitter pain settled in his heart.

They were driving along the road that passed near Sazli-dere when they saw someone running down the hill, shouting at them. The Commissioner felt a twitch of apprehension. What were they up to now? . . . The man stopped ahead, waving his arms frantically. He would have been knocked over if Uncle Hamza had not been quick with the brakes. It was Memed Ali, panting and almost black with sweat. He ran up to the Commissioner and seized his hands.

'You go with blessings, my Commissioner,' he blurted out, his chest rising and falling like a bellows. 'All village bless you. Think of you for ever. Bless you for ever.'

The Commissioner could not say a word. The tears welled up and something knotted tight in his throat. They looked at each other. There was love, worship in the Kurd's eyes. Then Uncle Hamza pressed the accelerator. Memed Ali was left on the road shrouded in a cloud of dust.

It was some time before the Commissioner felt the knot in his throat loosen. The pain in his heart was lighter now.

'Memed Ali, Memed Ali,' he smiled. 'Memed Ali, Memed Ali!'

Then he started to whistle. It was the long-forgotten air from the Ninth Symphony.

On the Road

He threw the reins over the wooden boards of the cart and, his hands free now, emptied the contents of his pockets and started counting the money. The horses jogged on, heads hanging, hooves dragging in the dust of the road.

'Six sacks,' he calculated. 'At two liras each? Twelve . . .?' He counted the money again. 'Nine liras! Where can those three liras have gone to? I had some food, a sherbet too . . . But still . . . Oh well!' Impatiently, he shoved the money back into his pocket and lit a cigarette.

The road ran through dusty sun-scorched fields sown with cotton, sunflowers and maize. Now and again the cart would grind to a halt while the horses plucked tranquilly at the maize that hung, dark-green and mauve-tufted, from the stalks. Except for an occasional 'Gee-up, my pets!' the driver made no attempt to urge them on, and soon enough they would start off again.

The fierce noonday heat was upon them now. For all their slow leisurely motion, the horses were sweating heavily and the dust had caked on their wet hides. Even the driver's dusty face was streaked with runnels of sweat. He nodded drowsily.

'Gee-up,' he murmured mechanically as the cart jolted to a stop again.

Then he saw the woman. She was turning aside to make way for the cart. A mantle wrapped her from head to foot and her face was completely hidden. Her feet were bare and she stepped fitfully over the oven-hot dust of the road.

He motioned with his hand and she climbed into the cart and sat behind him.

'Gee-up, my children,' he said again and the horses resumed their slow, easy gait.

Farther up the road, a single mulberry-tree, white with dust, stood in a field, casting a dark inviting shade about it. Stirring to a trot, the horses left the road and made straight for the tree. The driver sat up as the cart came to a standstill in the shade, and glanced at the woman for the first time. She had so swathed herself in her mantle that he could not even make out her eyes. He took a small bundle from the feed-sack and opened it.

'Help yourself, sister,' he said.

The woman refused with a sign of her head.

He ate alone, unhurriedly. When he had finished, he rummaged in the feed-sack again and produced a paper bag of peaches that had turned to pulp in the heat. He selected a couple of the less crushed ones and offered them to the woman. She took them without a word, her back turned to him. He ate the rest of the squashed peaches, then leaned back and closed his eyes.

When he opened them again, the shadow of the mulberry-tree had shifted and the cart was in full sunlight.

'Gee-up, my pets,' he said, stealing a glance behind him. The woman was still there, in the same position as though she had never moved. For the first time since they had set out, he cracked his whip at the horses.

'Gee-up, my children. Gee!'

Back on the dusty road, the horses eased into their leisurely amble again.

The driver turned to the woman.

'Where are you coming from in this heat?' he asked.

'From the town,' she replied in a low voice.

Around them, spreading as far as the eye could see, the flat boundless expanse of brown ploughed land, green fields and yellow crops shimmered under the impact of the sun, and before them the lonely, dusty road uncoiled across the plain like a white ribbon.

'Which village are you going to?'

'To Kirmitli.'

'I'm from Hemiteh myself,' said the driver. 'That's two villages farther off.'

There was a silence. Then the driver began again.

'What did you go to town for in this heat?'

The woman did not answer. He thought she hadn't heard him and repeated the question. When she was silent again, he was angry, but his curiosity was aroused now.

'Is it a secret?' he asked at last.

She looked at him.

'No,' she said. 'Why should it be?'

The driver was a slim and wiry man with thick black brows. He wore black shalvar-trousers and a shirt of artificial yellow silk. His cap was new and set at a rakish angle.

'That good-for-nothing husband of mine,' said the woman in strained tones, 'he's divorced me. I had to go and get the papers from the Government.'

Little white clouds were dawning in the distance, far off in the south where the Mediterranean Sea was. A cool gust of wind blew from the west, stirring the dust of the road.

'Look here,' said the driver, 'you'll simply suffocate, wrapped up like that in this heat. Why don't you take that mantle off? Who's to see you on this lonely road?'

The woman shed the mantle with obvious relief, and the driver saw her for the first time. She had a heart-shaped face with large black eyes and full lips. Her face was flushed

scarlet and small beads of sweat had gathered on her long
slender neck. She was beautiful.

'Gee-up!' he shouted with sudden vigour.

He turned and gave her a long look. The woman dropped
her eyes.

'What's your name?' he asked.

'Emineh . . .'

'Well, Emineh, I must say that husband of yours is one
hell of a fool!'

'That he is, the good-for-nothing,' said Emineh. 'One
hell of a fool . . .'

The west wind was blowing steadily as they reached the
bridge at Karasu. There, the banks of the stream are over-
grown with tall, dense reeds. Suddenly, the driver lashed
the horses into the reed-bed. The cart lurched wildly and
the woman slipped back, almost falling out. Then it stopped,
unable to penetrate any farther into the thick wall of reeds.

'The horses can rest a while here,' said the driver. He was
breathing hard as he looked at her. She said nothing. He
swallowed. 'That husband of yours,' he said again, 'must
have been a hell of a fool. Why, if he'd been a man . . .'

'That he never was!' she said contemptuously. 'A weak-
ling, that's what he is, always under somebody's thumb.'

He jumped off the cart and started pacing about restlessly.
He plucked a reed, broke it into pieces and cast them off.
Then, like lightning, he had seized her hand.

'What's this?' she cried, shaking herself free. 'What d'you
think you're doing?'

He looked into her eyes.

'Don't!' he pleaded.

She jumped out of the cart and started walking towards
the road. The driver ran after her and caught her by the
waist.

'Are you mad, man?' she said, pushing him away and walking on.

'Look,' he said, following her. 'I've no one. No father, no mother, no wife. I'm all on my own. This horse and cart are mine. And I own three large fields in my village . . .'

She stopped. He grasped her tightly by the wrists again. His head was swimming with desire. The reed wall whirled about him and the whole world with it.

'Is that true?' she asked.

'I swear it is! And I've got cows too . . .'

'And you really have no one?'

'No one at all, no one! I'm just by myself . . .' He was dragging her into the reeds where it was dark and close.

When they emerged from the reed-bed, the west wind was blowing wildly, making havoc with the dust on the road. He swished his whip joyfully. The sleepy horses seemed to come to life again, and the cart trundled on in a whirl of dust.

They entered the village of Kirmitli at a spanking pace. He pulled up and looked at Emineh. Their eyes met. She was quite still.

'This is your village, Emineh, isn't it?' he said.

'Yes,' she said. She made no move to get out.

He turned and lashed the horses into motion. Raising a cloud of dust, the cart rolled swiftly on over the flat plain in the direction of the village of Hemiteh.

The Baby

He was walking so fast that the dust whirled up to his waist. The sun beat down on him, dulling his senses, and the red-hot earth seared into his torn shoes. He carried a baby wrapped in a patchwork shawl. The baby's head hung loosely over his right arm. Its eyes were closed and its face was as red as raw liver.

All about him, the fields were alive with toiling men and women and the drone of harvesting machines throbbed in his ears. He turned off the road and set the baby down in the shade of a water-cart. Then, dipping the mug, he drained it in one long, thirsty draught.

A thin-faced woman with a pointed chin came up to the cart for a drink. She stopped and her black eyes widened with recognition.

'Why, Ismail, brother! What brings you here?' Her glance fell on the baby. She picked it up quickly. 'Alas,' she said, 'its neck is drooping so . . . How can it live, brother, after . . . Poor Zala, my dark-eyed Zala . . . There was no one like her.' She thrust her breast into the baby's mouth. 'Look, Ismail, brother! The child wants the breast. It's hungry, that's what's wrong with it. The heat has sucked it dry. I'm going to call Huru. Her breasts are bursting full, while her own baby whines away helplessly at home. Hey there, Huru! Huru, my girl, come here. Hurry!'

A young woman detached herself from a group of men and women who were binding sheaves farther off.

'Look, Huru! Zala's baby. Come and suckle it.'

Huru took the child and turned away.

'It's fate, poor mite,' she said. 'My breasts were so swollen, I couldn't stand it any longer. There I was, just about to spill my milk on to the ground . . . It's fate . . .'

'There was no one like Zala,' said the woman with the peaked chin. 'We used to go hoeing together when we were girls. She had a gay, smiling face. And her hair! So thick and long . . . Black, almost blue, it was. She was always a little delicate, though. D'you remember? She couldn't bear to go barefoot. She would tie some rags about her feet . . .

'Poor Zala!' said Huru. 'Who would have thought her child would be left like this among strangers?'

The baby's eyes were closed and only its chin moved. There was milk smeared around its mouth.

Some of the women, who had seen the baby in Huru's arms, joined them.

'What!' cried old Hava, whose white hair hung out from her torn headkerchief. 'Is it Zala's baby?' Her eyes filled with tears. 'Alas, my dark-eyed Zala! How can it be she's dead. . . .'

'How did she die, Ismail?' asked Black Elif, a squat, hollow-cheeked woman. 'Wasn't there anything you could do?'

Ismail's head was bowed. Suddenly he snatched the child out of Huru's arms.

'She died,' he answered sharply. 'I took her to the doctor, but she died. He gave her injections, but she died.'

He walked away quickly, his torn black shalvar-trousers swinging about his long legs.

The women stared after him. Old Hava's shrivelled lips moved softly.

'How he grieves, the poor man! He's crying tears of

blood. He couldn't look us in the face. As if it was he who killed her . . .'

'Oh, come now, woman!' cried Black Elif. 'He simply neglected her, may he be struck down! Let him wander about like this with the child in his arms from village to village. Let him! He never took her to the doctor, not for twenty days he didn't. They say the placenta didn't come out. Just rotted inside her . . . Was there anybody like Zala? Why, if Big Emineh hadn't died, would she have given her daughter to that Ismail who came from God knows where?'

'Poor man,' said Huru. 'He's left to the mercy of strangers. He's a good honest man, Ismail. He never did anybody any harm.'

'Will he find someone to nurse the child?' wondered old Hava.

'There's no one,' said the woman with the peaked chin. 'People can hardly look after their own children now. Look at Huru! She has to leave her pretty child at home where it whines all day long like a hungry animal, while she spills her milk on the ground here. Yes, Huru's child is in a bad way, for when she comes home in the evening her milk is like blood . . .'

'What can I do?' cried Huru. 'We'd all go hungry if I didn't work. We'd be left to the charity of strangers. It isn't as if you didn't know this, sister. If I could help it . . .'

'It's hard,' said old Hava. 'To depend on charity is worse than death.'

'And your mother-in-law,' pursued the woman with the peaked chin. 'She's blind. How can you leave the child with her?'

'She adores it, and she has a way with children. If a child has been crying its eyes out and won't stop, just take it to her. It'll calm down at once. Such lullabies she sings . . .'

'Yes,' said Black Elif. 'But suppose the child's face is covered with flies, that it's being eaten by them? It has to cry or she won't know. What can she do, poor woman? She loves children, but she's blind. They say that more often than not, she thrusts the milk bottle into the child's eye instead of its mouth . . .' She looked after Ismail. Where's he going now? she wondered. Where is he taking the child? Who will care for it?

'There's his uncle,' said old Hava. 'He'll do something.'

The woman with the peaked chin was making her way back to the labourers.

'Huh!' she said over her shoulder. 'And where's the woman to nurse it there? God forbid that a baby live on after its mother!'

'Oh my God!' cried old Hava, 'why didn't you let it die when its mother died? Did you need this orphan to help fill the world? Poor Ismail! With everyone busy in the fields, what will he do?'

The sun was high in the sky now and the huge plain was ablaze, gleaming like a burnished copper plate. The shining metal of a harvesting machine flashed near by, dazzling Ismail. His eyes were burning with sweat. Then he saw a single mulberry-tree, white with dust, on the edge of the road. He laid the baby under its scanty shade and, taking off his shirt, wrung it out and spread it on a blackberry bush barely visible from the dust. The baby was crying. Black flies swarmed over its face and eyes. With a swift motion, Ismail waved them away, but the baby did not stop. He took it up in his arms again and started rocking it to and fro.

'Hush, little one,' he said softly. 'Hush, hush-a-by . . .'

But the whining continued. He snatched up the wet shirt

from the bush, put it on hurriedly and strode away. The
baby was still crying, almost moaning, in a thin small voice.

A truck passed them by, leaving a long, blinding trail of
dust. When Ismail emerged from the dust, a pungent smell
of swamp came to his nostrils. On his right stretched a
green rice-paddy, steaming under the burning sun. The
stagnant water in the roadside ditch was skimmed with
creamy dust. On the edge of the paddy stood an aged field-
hand, white-bearded and bent, an *aba* thrown over his
shoulders and a hoe in his hand.

'Hey there, wayfarer!' cried the old labourer. 'The child's
head is hanging.'

Ismail did not seem to hear him. His head bowed, he
passed on quickly.

'God protect us,' muttered the old labourer to himself.
'He's fallen on evil days, that one . . . Left with a baby . . .'

Ismail entered the village without slowing his pace, almost
running along the narrow dusty lane where dung had been
heaped into tall piles. His uncle's house was only a grass-
roofed hut with sagging reed walls. Near the door was an
old cart, its paint peeled off and its wheels rusted. Under it
sprawled a yellow dog, its long red tongue lolling out. A
few open-beaked hens were wriggling about in the dust. The
door was open and an old woman sat on the threshold, fast
asleep, her legs drawn up and her head resting on the door-
jamb.

Ismail stopped before the door, his eyes still fixed miserably on the baby. The old woman slowly lifted her head at
the sound of the baby's crying.

'Why Ismail, my child!' she exclaimed, suddenly wide
awake. She rose and took the child from him. 'Hush, little
one. Hush, don't cry. Come in, Ismail, It's sweltering out
there. Come, come. Oh, my poor luckless one!'

Ismail was staring at her with glassy eyes.

'Ismail, my son,' she said, touching his arm, 'come in. You're drenched with sweat. Drenched . . .'

He followed her inside and sank down on the dirt floor as if all the strength had suddenly been drained out of his legs.

She laid the baby on a ragged mat and turned to him.

'My child,' she said, 'don't torment yourself so. Life is like this. You can't die with the dead. Zala was a good wife, I know, but you must pull yourself together now. Where is the man who doesn't lose his wife, the wife who doesn't lose her husband? One in a thousand, my child. Stop tormenting yourself. You can't change what is. You must bear it. Think of yourself now. We've been so worried about you. He takes the baby in his arms, Ismail, they told us, and sings to it all the time . . . Night and day, like one possessed, he keeps singing lullabies. Don't do this, my son. Don't do this to yourself.'

Ismail's long face had grown longer and darker. His eyes seemed to have turned in their sockets.

'Aunt,' he said, 'dear Aunt Jennet, it's killing me. Make it stop crying. Do something.'

She picked up the child.

'Hush, little one, hush, poor orphan . . . Hush, my hapless one. Hush-a-by . . .'

Her hair was white with a yelllow strand here and there and she had small bright eyes. A large strong chin lent a masculine look to her face.

'Hush, my hapless one,' she murmured, as she walked up and down, rocking the baby in her arms. 'Hush-a-by, my orphan. Hush-a-by . . .'

The child cried as though it had been wound up.

'They say, Ismail, that Zala died through want of proper care. They say you took her to the fields, heavy as she was with child, right up to the last day. And when the pains started you cast her into a stable, with no one to assist her . . . All alone you left her. That's what they're saying about you, may they be punished for their gossiping tongues!'

A shadow fell across the threshold and a bright-faced young girl came in. She had narrow shoulders and her plump hips were outlined under her black shalvar-trousers. Her eyes were huge below the thick matted brows and the shadow of her lashes fell on her dimpled face. She took the baby from Jennet and, turning away from them, bared her breast and put it in the child's mouth. It stopped crying.

Outside, two little boys, stark naked, crept up to the door. Each held a knife in one hand and a twig in the other. Their bellies were large and swollen and their necks as thin as sticks. One of them stuck his head in at the doorway, then drew it back quickly.

'Hist!' he whispered. 'If you saw!' He lifted a finger. 'It's neck is that thin . . .'

The other boy also stole a look inside.

'It really is that thin . . . As thin as a straw. Little sister Döndü is suckling it.'

'But not for real, you know. Girls don't have milk. Not unmarried girls who don't go with a man. My mother said so. She's just making believe . . .'

'Well, what if it is make-believe? The baby's not crying. It's happy, isn't it?'

They walked away, whittling at their twigs.

'That's what they're saying about you, Ismail. They say you locked her in there with the baby, and not a soul to give them even a drink of water, while you went to the fields. Ah, Ismail, you know how tongues wag. If one won't believe it, a thousand will. A man's mouth is not a sack you can draw shut by pulling a string. Why, people are just ready to tear

you to pieces the minute you have troubles. They say that
in that dark room poor, sick Zala would take up her child in
her arms and turn about stark naked, like one demented.
May they be punished for their gossiping tongues! They
say she went mad with grief . . . Ah, Ismail, my child . . .'

Ismail, who had seemed not to be listening, suddenly sat
up.

'Aunt,' he said, 'for heaven's sake . . .' His voice was
pleading, but angry. 'For God's sake, Aunt, d'you think I'd
ever hurt Zala's little finger? She was the mainstay of my
home. The mainstay . . . Ask me what happened. Ask me
what I feel. Let them talk. You ask my heart. It's burning
inside me like a live coal. How can I stop grieving for Zala,
ever? Of what use am I now she's gone? Can I ever find another one like her, even if I walk the whole world over?
Can I? Ask me how I feel!'

Jennet's eyes filled with tears.

'There was no one like Zala,' she said. 'Never anyone
like her in this world . . .'

Ismail's voice seemed to come not from him, but from the
wall, the floor, some other place. His eyes were half-closed.

'Aunt,' he said, 'you must believe me, it wasn't my fault.
"Zala," I said, "your time's drawing near. Stop working in
the field now. I can do the rest of the threshing alone. Anyway, there's so little left to be done . . ." So little left there
was, but she wouldn't listen to me. "I've been waiting and
waiting for this day," she said. "To be free at last! To work
for myself and not for strangers! I'll work till I drop dead,
till my bones break. It's only this year," she said, "that at
last you're no longer a mere field hand. How many years
have I waited for this day! To work another's field as a
partner instead of as a field hand! Think! Half the crop will
be ours." Nothing I said could make her stay at home.

She was already heavy, her belly was huge. It made my heart bleed to see her work. "Zala, don't," I begged her. "Don't do this." But she persisted. "This is what I've always wanted. How many times have I not said to myself, will I ever see the day when I'll work on my own and not for others? How many years have I toiled miserably in the houses of strangers?" She put all her heart and soul into her work. "This is what I've been waiting for," she kept saying. "My father was a field hand, my mother a servant, and they died without seeing anything better. I'm not going to be like them." Like one possessed, she kept repeating, "This is what I've been waiting for . . ."

'That day, it was so hot, Aunt, the birds just dropped, crack, from the skies, their tongues hanging out. We were carrying our wheat to the threshing floor. The sun was high in the sky, boring into our heads like a nail, and Zala had lifted a huge sack on to her back. Two men would barely have been able to lift it. "Zala," I said, "you mustn't load yourself like this." But her eyes filled. "This is what I've been waiting for . . ." Suddenly, halfway to the threshing floor, she threw down the sack. "What is it?" I asked. "The pain," she replied. "It's getting worse. This morning it wasn't so bad, but now it's getting sharper. It's like a knife. I'll go home. You mind your work. Don't stop. We mustn't let the ants get a share of our crop. Our own crop . . ." She turned to the village holding her belly with her two hands. But after a few steps she dropped down. I rushed to her side. "You go right back," she cried. "D'you want the ants to eat up our crop? I can walk home all right." She got up and walked away.

'When I came back that evening, she was lying down, and by her side, wrapped up in old rags and laid in a sieve, was the baby. She had cut the cord herself with a pair of

blunt scissors. There wasn't a woman to assist her at the
farm. All by herself, she had washed the child and put salt
over it and laid it there . . .

'Well, Aunt, there they were, the Agha on one side, Zala
on the other, biting my head off. "D'you want the birds
and ants to eat away our crop?" they said. The Agha was
angry and shouted at me, and Zala kept repeating: "We've
been lucky to get this chance, a chance in a million, to have a
crop of our own. You can't leave it to rot there because of me.
I can look after myself." She harried me so, there was
nothing I could do about it. I had to go to the field, leaving
her there all by herself.'

Jennet sighed quietly.

'She had always toiled for others. Without a father . . .
To have something of her own seemed to her sweeter than
life. She didn't live to see it. Alas, my poor Zala, she didn't
live . . .'

Ismail continued unheeding.

'She had been in bed for a week without being able to get
up, when I said to her: "Zala, you can't go on like this.
You'll never get well this way." Her face was like wax, her
bones jutted out . . . "I'll wait by your side and look after
you," I said. "And if you're not better I'll take you to the
doctor. What do I care about the crop, what do I care about
anything when you're like this." She began to cry, begging
me to go on with the work. "I'll be all right in the morning,
you'll see," she said. She sent me back to the field and remained there all alone, with nobody to bring food or water, in
a wretched state. If it weren't for Zeki Agha, I'd have got
the better of her, but the Agha, curse him, was pressing me.
"I took you into partnership," he said, "when you were only
a common hireling. You've no right to let my crop rot in the
fields." In the evening, I'd come home. "Zala," I'd beg

her, "you're not well. Let me stay beside you or let's go to the doctor." And every time she'd swear to God she was better. "Today I feel a little better," she would say. "In the morning I'll get straight out of bed." And I'd come back in the evening to find her still lying there. Twenty days had passed and Zala had grown paper-thin. Her eyes had sunk into their sockets. She was just skin and bones. There was not so much work left now. But I had had enough. I couldn't bear it any longer. I saw I was losing Zala . . . I was losing her!'

His lips began to tremble, but his voice hardened. It was under control now, strong and firm, no longer a murmur.

'I went and planted myself before Zeki Agha. "Agha," I said, "my wife is dying. I must take her to the doctor." The Agha laughed. "Ismail," he said, "don't you know our women? They lie and lie in bed, sick beyond hope you'd think, but they always get over it in the end. They don't need doctors. They're tempered steel, they are. What are you worrying about? You go on with your work." "No," I said. "Agha, whatever I have let it be yours, yours as your mother's milk. My cotton, my sesame, my wheat, I give everything to you freely. Let it be yours. But get me twenty-five liras." He yielded finally, and gave me the money. I found a cart and took her to town, but the doctor wasn't there. He had gone away on leave. I searched the town from end to end. There was a health officer, one of those who give quinine injections. He came out, gave one glance at Zala and leaned over to my ear. "But she's done for," he whispered. "You give her a shot," I said. "I can't," he said. "It's no use." I took out the money. "Here," I said, "is your money. Give her the injection. I'm paying you, aren't I? You'd do it to my horses, to this tree, if I paid you to. What is it to you? Give her this injection brother," I said, "so that my conscience may be at rest, so that people should not cover me with curses, so that friend and foe should see." He was a good man and gave her an injection. "Give her another one, brother, I owe such a lot to Zala . . ." He gave her another one. Her skin was stuck to her bones . . . Just skin and bones, Aunt, that's what Zala had become. If you'd seen her with your own eyes, you'd have said, "This isn't Zala."

'It was midday when I hitched the horses to the cart. The world was crackling in the heat as we started for home. If she's to die, I thought, let it be at the farm. It was so hot, so unbearably hot. The huge plain, the whole world was ablaze. We had hardly gone half the way, when Zala sat up erect all of a sudden. She was going to say something, but her head fell back. I heard her murmur: "A chance in a million . . . My child . . ." So softly, so low . . .'

'A chance in a million she had, poor thing, to work on her own,' said Jennet. 'But fate . . . Alas, alas Zala . . .'

'Her eyes turned. There was no sound, no breath. The child was in her arms. The sun was drilling into my head. I felt strange. Then everything went black. When I came to myself, I was lying on the ground, covered with dust, aching all over. Not a trace of the cart or the horses. I started up and ran. If the horses have upset the cart into a stream, I thought . . . Alive, all she ever had was misery and toil. Dead, I thought, let her body not be disgraced. The child, I thought, must not fall prey to birds and worms. If it must die . . . And it will. Can a baby live without its mother? It's difficult enough to keep a baby alive even when it has its mother . . .

'As I ran, I looked about to see if the child had not fallen somewhere along the road. I ran and ran. And then I saw a crowd gathered in the centre of a village. What village?

I still don't know which one. Just a village . . . I heard the word "dead" and I broke into the crowd. The cart was there, and the child still in Zala's arms, its face covered with dust, its eyes closed. The women were weeping. I climbed into the cart and drove away. They didn't ask me: "Who are you? What is the dead woman to you?" They didn't ask me: "Where are you going?" Not a word passed their lips. They just stared like stones.

'I was left with the baby. Harvest time . . . Everybody busy . . . I took it to a neighbouring village where there was a woman who had milk and left it with her. Two days later they brought it back to me. She would not suckle it any longer. "I've hardly enough for my own child," she had said. "I can't kill my own child to feed a stranger's." There isn't a nursing mother in the whole neighbourhood that I didn't try. They all dumped it back into my arms. With all the work in the fields, there I am, bound hand and foot. On one side a child whining all the time like a hungry kitten, on the other the crops. I'm at my wits' end.'

He stood up. He was so tall his head touched the grass roof of the hut. He swayed and sank down again.

'So you see how it is,' he said. 'You are another mother to this child. Help me! What shall I do?'

Jennet, her head bowed, sat motionless.

'Ismail,' she said, 'this was a chance in a million to work for yourselves, but she didn't live to see it. That's what Zala wanted to say, Ismail. "Take care of my child," is what she was going to say . . .'

'She said it all the time,' said Ismail. 'A chance in a million, a chance in a million . . . She was so happy . . .'

The young girl Döndü walked up to Jennet without taking her breast from the baby's mouth. Her face was aflame.

'Aunt Jennet,' she whispered, bending to her ear, 'when

the baby's sucking I feel all strange. I feel pleasant things
down my back. I wish it would suck like this all day. I
wish there were ten babies to suckle like this. It's so pleasant . . .'

'Don't be silly!' said Jennet. 'It does that to all of us.'

Towards evening Ismail's uncle, a large hulking man,
came home. Bits of straw, husks of wheat and dust clung to
his sunburned face.

'Ismail!' he exclaimed. 'We heard about your mis-
fortune and our hearts bled for you . . .'

The baby was lying on a blanket at the foot of the central
prop of the hut. It was crying.

'Man,' cried Jennet, 'send for Musdulu. His wife is
suckling now. So is Emineh, the lame woman. There's
Huru too, but she can hardly tend to her own child, poor
thing. Musdulu's wife has plenty of milk and she's clean.
Send somebody to Musdulu. His wife told me that if he
agrees, she'll suckle it.'

Musdulu arrived a little later with the boy sent to fetch
him. He sported a flashy red kerchief over the collar of his
navy-blue coat and a brand-new cap over his carefully
combed hair. His shalvar-trousers were new too.

The uncle took him by the hand and made him sit
down.

'My son,' he began, 'my good Musdulu . . .' He pointed
to the baby crying beside the prop. 'You see . . . God
protects us all.   Man is a creature of many woes, but if he
were not in need, God wouldn't reach out to help him. Your
wife has plenty of milk. Ismail will spare nothing. He will
give unstintingly. What do you say? A good deed is never
lost. Do a good deed and throw it into the ocean and if the
fish don't know it, God will . . . Do a good deed, God will
know.'

Musdulu's head was bowed, his thin lips pursed tightly. He was silent.

'My son,' the uncle began again, 'you know it's harvest time. No one at home. No women, no children to help. That's how it is with Ismail. Just imagine it, he's got no one, the poor man. He's had a chance in a million to work on his own. We can't let him lose it because of the child. What do you say, Musdulu? Don't you have anything to say, my son?'

Musdulu did not raise his head. He was very still.

'It isn't every day one has a chance to do a good deed,' the uncle persisted. 'You can be sure God will bless you for it. You'll be opening the gates of Paradise for yourself, because if your wife doesn't give it milk this child will die. It's a life you'll be saving. Look how it cries, poor mite . . . Can a man's heart be deaf to it?'

Musdulu rose and walked to the door. One foot over the threshold, he turned.

'Veli Agha,' he burst out, 'what made you take Musdulu's wife for a servant? My wife is not a servant!'

He stalked off in a fury.

Ismail sprang to the door, his hand stretched out.

'Brother!' he cried. 'Brother, don't! It's wicked.'

His uncle gripped his arm.

'Man!' he said. 'Don't go begging this son of a bitch. Why, you're like a woman! What's come over you? Let it die, man.' He pointed to his wife. 'This woman has buried sixteen children. Not babies like this one, but fine healthy babies.'

'My child,' said Jennet, 'you're not yourself. A baby . . . Not a month old! You'll marry. God will give you others. If it has to die, let it die. Sixteen I've given to this hard earth. How did I bear it? A barren hearth . . . You'll marry again, Ismail. Don't worry so, my child. You'll make yourself ill.'

Ismail's face was white as chalk. Jennet's expression changed as she looked at him.

'Wait a minute,' she said. 'Let me see . . . Emineh, the lame woman, one . . . Huru, two . . . Emineh, one . . . Huru . . . There just isn't anyone else. But Emineh's milk is poisoned. Not one of her children ever lived. Why, as far back as I can remember, she's been bearing children. Each year she bears one, and each year it dies before it's a month old. She herself doesn't know how many children she's had up to now. How can I give her the child? As for Huru, she's head over ears in her own troubles. Her own child's got diarrhoea after sucking and sucking its mother's milk, all hot from the day's work in the fields. She leaves it to the blind woman. Blind! How can she care for the child?'

'Woman,' said the uncle impatiently, 'what are you sitting there muttering for? Poisoned or not, there isn't anyone but this lame woman. We've got to give her the child.'

'But man,' protested his wife, 'it would be nothing better than killing it on the spot! You can't do that. In cold blood. . .'

'Aunt,' Ismail broke in, 'if she'll take it, let's give it to her. Let it not die of hunger at least.'

They sent for the lame woman. She came hobbling along, up down, up down, trailing her lame leg behind her, a short woman whose body fell so heavily to one side that it was a wonder she did not topple over. She wore faded black shalvar-trousers, so old that if one thread were pulled out, they would surely fall to pieces. Pieces of dough clung to her clothes. Her eyes disappeared beneath a mop of dirty hair, and huge moles sprouted all over her black, wrinkled face.

She planted herself before the uncle.

'Veli Agha,' she said, 'you sent for me. Here I am.'

'My daughter,' said the old man, 'you see this baby. I sent for you to nurse it. Ismail will do anything you want. He'll give to your heart's content. To your heart's content... It's a life you'll be saving, which is no little deed. God will love you all the more for it. What do you say, my daughter?'

'Sister,' said Ismail pleadingly, 'whatever you want I'll give to you. Even if you ask me for bird's milk, I'll find it for you.'

Emineh's face became even darker and more shrivelled.

'Veli Agha,' she said, 'my milk's not enough for my own child. Do I ever eat properly to have milk?'

Ismail straightened.

'Look,' he said, 'my own sister Emineh, even if it's bird's milk you want, I'll find it for you. What do you say? Come on, say yes.'

'What can I say, brother?' replied Emineh. 'When my man comes home this evening, we'll see.'

And without giving any milk to the baby crying on the ground, she turned and left.

The young girl Döndü came running in. She took up the child and, turning her back to them, gave it the breast. The crying stopped.

'This mother of mine!' she complained. 'She won't let me go out. She just invents work for me on purpose! This mother of mine . . .'

The croaking of frogs filled the night. The cool west wind, which had risen in the afternoon, had dropped now and the air was sticky, smelling of swamp and of fresh cow dung. The sky was studded with huge glittering stars.

Away from the house, on the edge of a meadow stood a tall

plane-tree. Every night white storks would settle on its branches, row upon row of white storks. The clatter of their beaks could be heard from time to time. Beside the uncle's house was a *chardak* for sleeping in the summer. The baby had been set in a cradle on one side of the *chardak* and there it lay crying persistently while old Jennet kept rocking the cradle. Uncle Veli had gone to sleep long ago and was snoring.

After a while the rocking cradle was still. Jennet must have fallen asleep too. It was long past midnight and the baby was still crying. Ismail tossed and turned on his mattress, shaking the whole *chardak*.

'Aunt,' he whispered at last, 'please take it to that lame woman now. It's killing me. It doesn't stop crying. It won't stop . . . Take it to her. Take it!'

The old woman sat up rubbing her eyes. She took the child from its cradle.

All the women in the village were talking of Emineh, the lame woman, and of Ismail's baby. Working in the fields, grazing their animals, weaving at their looms, whenever two women got together, they could speak of nothing else.

That evening, a group of women had gathered at Black Elif's door and were twirling their hand spindles as they talked.

'Eh, my dear, this is what I call luck! Did you ever see the like of it? Zala's death was a boon for that sluttish Emineh.'

'Why, my dear, if she'd at least do what she's paid for! All day long that child whines away like an abandoned puppy, and she sits there like a lady stuffing herself with all the food Ismail brings. He's as good as emptied the market of sugar and butter, the fool, and filled her home with goods. That lame woman's house has become a real shop!'

'Eh, a real shop!'

'I can't bear to pass her door. All day long, it cries and cries, the poor mite. Like a little puppy . . .'

'Poor innocent babe . . . It breaks my heart!'

'If you see Ismail . . . All pale and wan . . .'

'It breaks my heart!'

'Everything he has, even the shirt on his back, will be swallowed up by that lame woman. He'll soon find himself a field hand again.'

'That child's in a bad way.'

'It'll die . . .'

'Why, rather than give it to that lame woman, he'd much better have left it under a tree!'

'To be carried away by the eagles . . .'

'Much better have thrown it into the river!'

'Buried it alive straight away . . .'

'Yes, my dear!'

'Every other day he comes with a sack on his back. For the woman to eat, he says, for her to have more milk . . .'

'He sits by the cradle, staring at the child, without saying a word . . .'

'His heart is broken, poor man.'

'Broken . . .'

'Motherless . . .'

'How can a baby live without its mother?'

'Poor Ismail! All his efforts are in vain.'

'Her milk's poisoned.'

'If her own children had lived . . .'

'It won't live.'

Ten days after she had taken in the child, Emineh roused the whole village with her lamentations.

'Aaah, women!' she screeched. 'I never saw the like of it.

They've dumped that child on me. It never has its fill of milk. Always hungry for more . . . It's my own child who's getting the worse of it. He's got diarrhoea now. Like water it's coming out. He'll die, my Duran. He would have lived, I know it, and now, because of the other one, he'll die. I'll take their child and dump it right back on them, I will! Let him keep his gifts. What does he bring anyway? Here I am, killing my own child, and he gives me two pounds of sugar. Two pounds of sugar in ten days! Yes, my dear, two pounds of sugar . . .'

'Take it back to Jennet,' the women urged her. 'Take it back.'

After Emineh had gone, trailing her lame leg behind her, they turned to each other.

'The child won't live anyway.'

'Let her take it back!'

'All day it whines, like an abandoned puppy . . .'

'Why, Emineh will kill it before its time!'

'Let her take it back!'

'Did you hear, my dear? She doesn't like what he brings her!'

'Eh, the more one has . . .'

'Two pounds of sugar! Why, that slut hasn't had that much sugar since she dropped out of her mother's womb!'

'That lame slut . . .'

'How I pity that man! It's heart-rending.'

'Let her take it back!'

Two days later, Ismail came again with a sack full of goods on his back. Without stopping at his uncle's, he walked straight to Emineh's house. It was a one-room hut roofed with rotted grass, the colour of lead. Its brush wall was plastered with lumps of dung. Inside, there was next to nothing: three sacks dumped in a corner and a worn-out mattress shedding its cotton. A calf was tethered in another corner and next to it was the cradle, a dirt-blackened, cracked old thing, in which the two babies lay side by side, their little fists thrust into each other's faces. The place smelled of fresh dung and urine. Under the window, which was hardly larger than a hand, stood two moss-covered pinewood jars oozing water.

Ismail stopped dead at the foot of the cradle. He stared.

'Sister . . .' he said. 'Sister Emineh, what's happened to the child?'

The baby's skin was stuck to its bones. Its belly had swelled and its eyes were sunk deep in their sockets.

Ismail could stand it no longer. He went out.

Emineh shook the sack he had brought.

'Look!' she cried. 'Look, Elif, my girl! Just two pounds of sugar . . . He expects me to nurse it on that, the devil take him, and he has the cheek to stand there, giving himself airs, and ask what's happened to the child!'

As she spoke, she took the things from the sack and threw them all over the place.

'It'll die! My child will die. Diarrhoea! It'll die and everybody will blame me!'

'Well, take it back then!' exclaimed Black Elif. 'Why do you keep it any longer?'

'My child'll die!' she howled. 'Everybody'll say she killed her own child in order to nurse a stranger's!'

Ismail straightened from the brush wall against which he had been leaning.

'Bitch,' he said, the word hissing through his lips. 'Lame bitch!'

He walked off, swaying as if drunk.

Two days later, Emineh, shouting and cursing at the top of her voice, brought the baby back to Jennet.

'What will people say?' she kept repeating, 'if my own child dies? What will people say?'

Jennet sent the child back to its father.

The wheat was heaped on the threshing floor to the height of a man. Ismail had started threshing long before dawn. The sun was now quarter high and the mound in the centre was rising steadily. He threw his fork on to the stalks and took a long drink from the jug which stood in a shady spot of the threshing floor. On the thresher, a young boy with a slender neck and very long eyelashes kept lashing a whip at the two lean bay horses, as he led them rapidly round and round over the yet unbroken stalks. The air smelled rankly of straw and dry grass.

Ismail leaned over the baby, who had been crying in the shade of the wheat rick, and thrust into its mouth a raki bottle filled with milk to which he had fixed a nipple. The child stopped crying and started to suck weakly. Ismail's face was covered with straw and dust. His breath came out in gasps as though through a bellows.

'Mehmet,' he called to the boy, 'come along and eat.'

Mehmet left the horses near the wheat so that they should eat too. He came up and opened his bundle of food.

Ismail was eating with one hand, while he held the bottle with the other. If he so much as made a move to pull the bottle away, the baby would start crying at once, and Ismail could not bear that.

The boy talked all the time as he ate.

'Uncle Ismail, let me tell you something. There was a boy in our village.' He pointed to the baby. 'Just like this one. His mother had died, and everywhere the father went, he

had to carry the baby with him. He was poor, you see, and
no one wanted to look after the baby. It was dying of hunger, crying and crying . . . My mother said so. She said it
was dying in its father's arms. Now that boy, you know, they
call him the Kurd's son in the village, but my mother says
his father wasn't a Kurd or anything . . . One night his
father wrapped the baby up in an old sack, put it on the
fountain stone in the middle of the village and left it there.
Then he just disappeared. A Kurdish girl found the child
and brought it up. So they call him the Kurd's son. His
father never set foot in the village again. No one knows
where he went, no one ever saw him again. Oh, I don't
know! That's what my mother says, anyhow . . .'

Ismail suddenly stood up. The bits of straw stuck to the
hairs of his chest flashed in the sunlight. He seized the child
and walked away.

The blind woman heard the sound of steps and turned her
head towards the door.

'Who's that?' she cried. 'Who is it? Have you got a baby
with you?'

'It's me, Mother,' said Ismail.

'I'm sorry, my son,' said the blind woman. 'I don't
recognize your voice.'

'It's Ismail, Mother. Ismail of the Avshars. Durmush
Agha's old hireling . . .'

'Ah,' said the blind woman. Her voice was soft, but
bitter as poison. 'Every one of us grieved so for Zala. She
didn't live to see better days, poor girl. May that sluttish
lame woman be cursed! I've heard she wouldn't suckle the
child . . . Ah, if only my son were here! Huru wouldn't
go to the fields then, and I'd look after the baby for Zala's
dear sake. My son, it's crying there in your arms. Lay it

down in the cradle here, beside our little one. Have you done so? Hush, hush-a-by, my poor motherless lamb. Hush-a-by . . .'

She rocked the cradle to and fro.

'Mother,' Ismail said, 'when will Mahmud's time be up? How much longer . . .'

'Lulla-lulla-lullaby. Hush, hush, hush-a-by. Aaah,' cried the old woman with sudden vehemence, 'ah, my poor son! When it comes to taxes, does the Government ever lay off? Lulla-lulla-lullaby, hush, hush . . . I am an old woman and I never heard of a pardon, not once. Hush, my motherless lamb, hush-a-by . . . It's the road tax, Ismail. He couldn't pay it, and it grew and grew. Hush, my poor babe, hush, my little one . . . The Government says, let him give me my money, and I'll let him go . . . Hush, my love, hush. The Government says, if he doesn't pay me, he'll just rot in prison till he dies. Hush, my poor little one left among strangers, hush . . . And it's no little sum, my son. It can't be saved. Huru works, but what can one woman do alone? Time and time again I've said, I'll go and throw myself at the Government's feet. It's no use, they tell me, it's the money they must have. Hush, Zala's luckless baby, hush-a-by . . .'

The hut was just large enough to hold two beds side by side. Its brush wall was unplastered and the grass roof had grown so thin that the sun pierced through. It was spotlessly clean.

The blind woman was sitting near the door, her face turned towards the light. She was rocking the cradle very slowly and singing all the while.

'Lulla-lulla-lullaby . . . Motherless babies always cry like this, without stopping. Lulla-lulla-lullaby. Oh dear! I feel strange myself. My time is drawing near, it seems. Since

Mahmud went away, the fever's never left me, not a single day. It has me shaking all over and leaves me limp, exhausted. Hush, my love, hush, pretty flower of the mountains, don't cry, hush. Ah, if only my Mahmud were here, would I ever have let Zala's baby be dragged miserably like this from door to door! Hush-a-by, hush.' She stopped rocking the cradle. 'On which side did you put it, Ismail? Where is Zala's baby?'

Ismail took her hand and placed it on the baby. Her hand passed over the baby's face softly, caressingly.

'Alas,' she said, 'the poor motherless thing! Skin and bones it has become. Huru has finished gathering her crop. Now she's hoeing our cotton. Hush, hush-a-by. Skin and bones . . . Hush-a-by.'

The sun had set when Huru came home. She took in the situation immediately. Her mother-in-law was lying down, groaning and shivering. The fever came over her like this every afternoon. Ismail was sitting by the cradle rocking it slowly to and fro.

Huru seemed to be twenty years old. Her face was tanned almost black from the sun.

'Ismail, brother,' she said. 'What can I say to you? My heart breaks for you, but what can I say? You see for yourself how it is. My breasts swell all day long, but I cannot suckle my own baby. I just press the milk out on to the earth. What can I say, Ismail, brother? If Mahmud were here . . .'

'Sister,' said Ismail, 'sister Huru, I'll give you anything you want. I'll do your threshing for you as soon as I've finished mine. You're my last hope.'

'Mother,' said Huru, 'what do you say? What can I say . . .'

'My daughter,' said the old woman, moaning all the while, 'my lovely black-eyed, golden-haired girl, we can't sit here and let it die. Why, it's almost dead already. Zala's baby . . . What can I say? Zala's keepsake . . .'

Ismail rose with a lightness in his heart for the first time in many days. He went out.

Huru carried the babies, one on each arm. The blind woman followed, her hand on Huru's belt. Dawn was just breaking when they reached the field. Huru made a little bed of grass and laid the children next to each other on it. Then she settled the blind woman near them.

The cotton field was about five acres wide. In the dim half-light it was not possible to distinguish the cotton from the other plants. As soon as it grew lighter, Huru started hoeing. There was not a single tree or shady spot in the field or anywhere near it. A smell of fresh earth rose at every blow of the hoe . . .

The sun was now high and heat enveloped the whole plain.

'Huru,' called the blind woman, 'the children are burning, my daughter. Come, my pretty child. Come and place them in my shadow.'

She was sitting with her back to the sun. Huru moved the two babies into her shadow.

'But Mother,' she said, 'at noon there'll be no shadow at all. What will we do then, Mother?'

The blind woman's lips trembled.

Her mouth was thin and drawn into a maze of wrinkles. Her face was as small as the palm of a hand, and two sunken little balls fluttered constantly under the closed eyelids. Her bony hands with the veins jutting out were dotted with small specks like sun spots. Sitting, she seemed no larger than a small child. When the babies cried, she would call to Huru to come and suckle them. Then swaying slowly from side to side, she would sing her lullaby.

> *'Sleep, my pretty baby, sleep, lulla-lulla-lullaby*
> *In lovely gardens you shall grow, lulla-lulla-lullaby.'*

Such a gentle voice the old woman had, a voice to soothe crying babes, a voice so full of warmth and compassion, it penetrated to the heart.

As the sun rose higher and higher, she leaned over the children more and more.

When the sun is at its zenith, scorching the huge plain, it is impossible even to touch the soil with the hand or to walk on the ground. The plants droop, the cotton leaves become limp. The blind woman then settled the children on her lap and huddled over them. One would have thought her asleep were it not for the lullaby she sang softly as she swayed slowly from side to side.

> *'Sleep, my pretty baby, sleep, lulla-lulla-lullaby*
> *In lovely gardens you shall grow, lulla-lulla-lullaby*
> *From your little green cradle, hush, hush, hush-a-by*
> *I've taken you, my pretty one, lulla-lulla-lullaby*
> *Poor motherless little babe, hush, hush, hush-a-by*
> *Never felt a mother's warmth, lulla-lulla-lullaby.'*

As she sang she stroked Zala's baby softly.

> *'Sleep, my pretty baby, sleep, lulla-lulla-lullaby*
> *In lovely palaces you shall grow, lulla-lulla-lullaby.'*

The sun beat down on them, the sun burned and con-sumed them, but the old woman managed to protect the two babies until the afternoon. It was just about five o'clock that the fever took her. She began to tremble and roll on the ground, shaking all over and writhing in long convulsions on the warm earth.

And so it was, day after day. The old woman keeping the two babies from the sun all through the long hot day, and in the afternoon . . .

They would continue like this until the hoeing of the five acres was through. There was just one little patch left, so little . . . But there was no help for it.

Bad news travels quickly. Ismail had finished threshing his crop and was stacking his grain when he heard it.

He found Huru lying down, her face yellow, her cheeks sunken.

'Sister,' he said, his voice coming out with difficulty, 'God help you. May she rest in peace. She didn't see the light in this world. May her grave be full of light . . .'

'She's dead,' said Huru in a tremulous voice. 'It's two days now . . . How she loved children! She had such a way of singing lullabies, it broke your heart . . .'

'May her grave be filled with light,' said Ismail softly. 'She never saw the light . . .'

'We have no *chardak*, brother, you know,' Huru moaned. 'Mosquitoes swarmed all over us where we lay on the ground. They say it was because of that . . . Ah . . .' She tossed her head. 'I'm burning, brother, burning all over . . .'

Ismail gazed at her silently. Then he said:

'Sister, I've brought you this.'

He put the sugar near her pillow. The children were sleeping peacefully in the cradle. He took up his baby and walked to the door. Then he turned back.

'Sister Huru,' he said, 'don't worry about your crop. I'll

do the threshing for you. Don't you have any fear in your heart for the crop. It isn't because I'm taking the child that . . .'

The shadow of a cloud passed over the dusty road. Far off towards the south, the white clouds that are called sails were gathering in clusters over the Mediterranean. As far as the eye could see, the huge level plain was turning blue under the late afternoon sun like a smooth calm sea. The dark shadows of the distant blue mountains were lengthening towards the east.

Ismail was up to his waist in whirling dust. On his left, the green rice-paddy stretched out to the village. A pungent smell of swamps reached his nostrils. In the ditch along the road the creamy film of dust covering the stagnant water broke into ripples as the wind swept over it.

The child's head rested on his right arm. Its sunken eyes were like two dark holes. Its neck was now so thin that it could not support its head, and its skin all shrivelled and black, was stuck to its bones. Its jaw hung slack and flies were swarming in and out of its open mouth.

Ismail's head was bent towards the baby. He kept looking at it as he walked.

Green Onions

This was the second time in his life he was taking a train. The first had been five years ago when he had left the village. He fidgeted with impatience as he sat on his bulky wooden suitcase, looking past the crowded platform to the empty railway lines. His hat, clothes, shoes, everything about him was shining new, as though he had just stepped out of a shop. His shirt especially caught the eye, a gaudy thing with large yellow stripes.

The train roared into the station spouting warm puffs of blue smoke. He snatched up the wooden suitcase, plunged into the jostling crowd and fought his way in. The corridors were jammed. People trod on his toes, he trod on theirs. At last, his face streaming red, his coat slipping off, he found himself before a compartment in which there were only a youth and a girl. A smell of fresh onions hung about the compartment. It made him think of spring and of new earth at home. He lifted the heavy suitcase on to the rack.

The girl's head rested on her companion's shoulder. She seemed to be sleeping. As the train pulled out of the station, she opened her eyes once and closed them again.

Suddenly he decided that he would buy green onions at the very next stop. Then he laughed the idea away. 'What's green onions? A whole field to pick from at home . . .' But still, at the station, he paid a whole twenty-five kurush for a bunch of green onions, thinking all the while of how the folks in the village would split their sides when he told them. The onions crunched crisp and fresh under his teeth, sweeter than they had ever tasted in his life. Only onions! Onions, insipid, unbearable when you had them day in day out, turning your mouth into a soapy lather bowl . . . And yet now . . .

Then he saw that the youth was staring at him fixedly. His eyes were large and sad and never moved from his face. He bent his head, but he felt the gaze weighing on him, sad and still. Annoyed, he bit into the onion and munched away vigorously. When he looked up again, the huge eyes were still on him. He picked a couple of onions from the bunch and held them out awkwardly.

'Here, brother,' he said. 'Have a bit too.'

The youth shook his head vaguely, while the girl lifted her head and gave him a blank, listless look.

'Have some, have some, brother,' he insisted. 'Let her eat some too. Green onions are good for the health. All green things are good, but green onions are best of all.'

The youth shook his head again, but his eyes were still glued on him.

He looked out of the window. They were speeding through a wide plain. Telegraph poles, a few trees, a dried-up torrent hurtled past and the sun-scorched grass flattened out as the train blasted by. Once, a single bare-boned cow flashed by, and then he caught a glimpse of a kite suspended high up in the sky. Then, there was nothing but the arid plain, empty and desolate.

His eyes met the huge frozen stare again. Why was he looking at him like that? Was it the deep scar left over from a scythe blow in that quarrel with Mistik Ali years ago? There was neither fear, nor pity, nor wonder in those eyes. Maybe it was the hat. There must be something wrong with it. He took it off and turned it about in his hands doubtfully. Then he clapped it back on his head. How thin the girl was! How parched and yellow her face, how laborious her breath . . . Before he knew it, he found himself talking very quickly.

'. . . Sick or something? Very pale, she is . . . Bad thing, sickness. Allah protect us all. But what can a man do? Cruel thing, sickness . . . Ties a man up hand and foot . . . What's ailing her?'

There was no reply.

'It can't be the fever,' he persisted. 'She'd have trembling fits . . . Nor chest trouble. She'd be coughing.'

The youth's eyes fell for the first time.

'She's just sick,' he said at last. His voice was low and dull. 'I took her to every doctor in the town. They couldn't make her well . . . All the village cures we tried, too. But still she wasted away . . . She's like this always. Half-conscious, asleep . . . It started a month after we got engaged. Three years ago . . .'

The youth's eyes were on him again, huge, dark, oppressive. God damn those eyes! What's he staring at me for like an ox, may his eyes drop out! . . .

'Yellow Mahmud, they call me . . .' The words poured out compulsively. 'Going back home now after five years. Came away to earn money for a team of oxen and now I have enough to buy ten!' He smiled proudly. 'Worked at heavy jobs in Izmir, I did. Made quite a wad. And now I intend to buy four oxen and four cows. Sheep too, brother, and goats. A horse and a mare . . . In that case you see there, I've got clothes for all the family, every one of them, the wife, the children, my old mother . . . Like a meadow bursting with spring flowers my house will be when I get back . . . Ah, brother, you should see our village! Pine-trees everywhere. The whole air smells of pines. And our water-springs! Each one a fountain of life . . .'

The youth seemed to come alive.

'Pine-trees,' he murmured. 'One doctor said she had the wasting disease. He said the pine air would do her good. But there are no pine-trees in our village. There are no trees at all . . .'

'Huge pine-trees we have,' said Mahmud proudly. 'The rich come from Marash and other towns to stay there in the summer.'

And then his heart gave a bound. The cold numb look had gone. The boy's eyes were on him, bright and eager. His face was flushed.

'Look here, brother!' Joy burst in him like a storm. His heart overflowed. 'Look, I've earned a mint of money, enough for ten oxen, not just a pair. Four cows I'm going to buy instead of one. Aleppo cows that yield bucketfuls of milk. We have plenty of honey too at home . . . The pine-trees . . .' He leaned forward. 'Look here, brother, take your betrothed and come straight to me. Come and I'll look after you both like the apple of my eye. She'll be as fit as a fiddle again in less than three months, I promise you. Reborn . . . And then I'll take charge of your wedding. We'll have it right there in the village. Come, bring her!' He seized the youth's hand and pressed it warmly. 'We'll make her eat *yalabuk*, fresh off the bark of the pines. All the youths of the village will gather it for her. They're good folks, our villagers are, you'll see! *Yalabuk*! There's nothing like it to bring a person back to life.'

The youth looked out of the window and nudged the girl.

'We're getting off at the next stop,' he said. 'Get ready, Döndülü. We're here.'

The girl sat up weakly and drew her shawl over her head.

The train grated to a stop. A flock of crows rose up from the small station building, cawing noisily.

The youth lifted the half-conscious girl on to his back.

'Our village is quite near,' he said as he went out. 'Behind that hill . . .'

Mahmud rushed after him and gripped his collar.

'If you don't come,' he said, 'I'll never forgive you, not in this world nor in the next. I'll be waiting for you day and night. Good-bye now. God bless you, brother.'

The train was now a place of joy. All the world was in tune with his happiness. Then he saw the eyes again, huge, insistent. The youth was staring up at him from the platform. He winced. The train stirred. Suddenly, like a flash, it dawned upon him.

'Hunu's the name of our village!' he shouted as the train moved away. 'Hunu village in the district of Elbistan. Hunu! Come to Marash and from there . . . I'll be waiting. Hunu! . . .'

He was still shouting as the train gathered speed, spurting clouds of warm blue smoke. Soon it was flying through the flat, boundless plain in a whirlwind of joy.

The Shopkeeper

In the centre of the village towers a massive old mulberry-
tree. Its trunk is so thick that two men cannot link hands
about it. At the height of summer when the whole of the
Chukurova plain swelters in the scorching heat, a man can
cool his steaming body in its dark, deep shade. Nestling
against this ancient tree is Mehmet Efendi's shop. It has
stood there over the years, always the same, with no refur-
bishing or extension except for an occasional reinforcement
of its sagging brushwood walls or a renewal of its reed roof.

Mehmet Efendi hails from the eastern Anatolian village of
Darendeh. He has tiny darting eyes and podgy white hands,
and over his huge paunch dangles a silver watch-chain at
least a yard long. This man from Darendeh is more an
integral part of the village than the natives themselves, and
indeed nobody remembers exactly when he first came. Some
say twenty years ago, others thirty . . . Once in a while one
of his children comes down from his village to visit him. The
child, always a different one, stays a few months with his
father and then leaves. He himself returns to his village
every couple of years. Then, he closes down, but in his
absence the villagers still come as usual and squat on the
little heaps of dung about the shop, staring dejectedly at the
time-bleached wooden door. It seems to them that the
village is not the same with the shop closed and Mehmet
Efendi not there.

During the months of June, July and August everyone is
away working in the fields. Only the old people and a hand-

ful of women and children remain in the village. The elders
are in the habit of drifting into the shop and settling down on
the low wooden benches that are fixed to the walls. There they
sit, passing the time of day and dozing until dusk when the
cattle come in from the pastures.

And there is the strange child, a boy of ten. He comes in
the minute Mehmet Efendi opens up. He has his own place
right opposite the door. There he sits, hunched and silent,
resting his chin on his short stick and listening to the old
men's talk. Nobody ever tries to make him go away. The
villagers have decided he must be a little mad and he has
already earned the nickname of Queer. Queer Sullu they call
him. No one in the village has ever been able to get a word
out of him. The only person he talks to at all is his mother.

At noontime the village is buried in a desolate silence,
broken only now and then by the distant braying of a donkey.
Nobody dares to venture out into the blinding sun. The
whole world is ablaze and sizzling, and even the dogs and
cats take refuge in the short noon shadow of the huts and
sprawl there with hanging tongues.

It is at just such a time that some barefooted woman
carrying an apronful of grain comes scurrying post-haste to
the shop, her wide red shalvar-trousers swelling out and her
face streaming with sweat. She dashes in and empties the
contents of her apron into one of the sacks in a corner.

'How much?' asks Mehmet Efendi.

'One peck.'

'What will you take?'

'I'll come in later on. You just write it down . . .'

And she rushes out again.

Mehmet Efendi scribbles something in the yellow book
before him.

There is not a woman in the village, who, behind her

husband's back, does not bring grain or flour to the shop in exchange for such knick-knacks as beads and necklaces, sweets and dried fruit, trimmings for her daughter's hope chest or slings for the boys. The currency between Mehmet Efendi and the women is not money but grain. Women are never given any money in the villages. And so they have to devise their own ways and means. The elders can be counted on to keep their own counsel and Sullu never opens his mouth. As for the daughters and wives of the elders, they send in their grain with another woman, and a slight sign is enough for Mehmet Efendi. He knows where the grain comes from and jots it down in his yellow book. Yes, there is a secret compact between Mehmet Efendi and the women. Still, it isn't as though the men don't know. They know it very well, but there is not much they can do about it. It is only at the onset of March, when the grain stocks run out, that the first anguished wails of women being soundly trounced rend the air. Curses rain down on Mehmet Efendi. But what can he do? Is he here to do business or not? How can he turn away a customer? What kind of sense is that? Well, the beating and howling persist until the first harvest at the beginning of May. And then the old pattern sets in again, and small measures of wheat and barley continue to find their way regularly into Mehmet Efendi's sacks.

A secret network links Mehmet Efendi's shop to every single house in the village. He is informed of the slightest event in the life of its inhabitants. Why has Osman quarrelled with his wife? Why does Veli slip daily and hourly off to that neighbouring village? Mehmet Efendi knows all, down to the last and most secret detail. He has to, in the interests of his profession . . .

The rider burst into the village at full gallop and dis-

mounted under the great mulberry-tree. He tethered his
sweat-blackened horse to a stake and strode into the shop
with a general greeting. Oily locks of black hair spilled out
from under his cap and he sported a yellow handkerchief in
his breast-pocket. His black shalvar-trousers were new but
dusty from the road.

He leaned over to Mehmet Efendi.

'All right about the girl, Uncle?' he whispered.

'Everything's ready,' replied the other in a barely audible
undertone.

They drew apart quickly.

'How's your father, my lad? And what's new in your
village? Is that gipsy creature still there? Or have you sent
him packing?'

'Nothing new,' shrugged the youth. 'Father's all right
and sends you greetings. As for the fellow, he's still there,
but not for long, you can be sure. We'll soon kick him out,
never fear.'

Mehmet Efendi was angry, but he kept a hold on himself.

'After Allah, I put all my trust in you, my young lion.
As for those ungrateful villagers . . .' He appealed to the
elders. 'Haji Agha, you tell me what you think of those
Yeriyokush people! Not one of them's so much as stepped
into my shop this twelvemonth! After all the credit I've
given them these many years . . . And why, I ask you?
Because some no-good pedlar tricks them into buying his
shoddies. He sells cheap, they say. Cheap! Why, I wouldn't
sell his wares for half the price! By Allah, I wouldn't! I just
couldn't. All the people hereabouts are like my own family.
I couldn't . . .'

'People don't count their blessings any more,' said Haji
Agha, his hands buried under his white beard. 'They have no

respect for their elders. Would Mehmet Efendi sell that kind of stuff?'

'I couldn't,' asserted the shopkeeper. 'I'd never be able to look the villagers in the face again if I did.'

'Those Yeriyokush people always were miserly,' commented another old man. 'You can't cook a good stew with bad meat.'

'In this village now,' pursued Mehmet Efendi, 'they'd make short work of such an outsider. We know how to stand by each other. It's a matter of honour. We . . .'

'Mehmet Efendi,' the youth broke in warmly, 'I've told you already that I'll deal with him. We wouldn't have put up with that vagabond either, but some people said he's only a poor beggar, let him earn his pittance too . . . Don't you worry about it. I'll have all of Yeriyokush buying from you again in no time. It's only because they said he was a poor beggar . . .'

'Valiant youth,' the elders murmured. 'He'll get back their custom for you, Mehmet Efendi, don't you worry.'

'Yes, yes,' said Mehmet Efendi. 'First Allah and then this valiant youth. I rely on him. But where did you get the idea the fellow was poor, my lad? Why, his kind would steal the nose off your face and you none the wiser. I know his kind, I do. Poor indeed! Ah, those villagers, heathens that's what they are! Forgetting how I helped them with credit when people around here hadn't so much as heard of a shop . . . And now they buy from this pedlar, robbing me of my livelihood at my age . . . What will my children eat? Destitute . . . Ah, they have no conscience!'

He had seized the watch-chain that dangled over his huge paunch and was pulling the watch out of his waistcoat-pocket and shoving it back again, in and out, in and out, without ever even glancing at it.

Queer Sullu, sitting as usual his chin on his stick, gazed silently at the shopkeeper. The elders said nothing. Myriads of flies hummed about the shop, swarming over the groceries and covering everything.

Mehmet Efendi's hand slowed down.

'I've a good mind to send them packing, all of them,' he said vindictively, 'and not give them so much as a crumb even if they pay me a million liras for it.'

He put the watch back into his pocket and went out to perform his ablutions.

'Old pimp,' growled one of the elders as soon as the shop-keeper's back was turned. 'Trying to take the bread out of a poor man's mouth, just because he sells his wares cheaper! Why don't you sell yours cheap too and people'll buy from you? But no, he has to build himself another couple of houses in Adana, the old miser!'

'Trying to do a poor fellow out of his bread . . .' concurred another.

Just then Mehmet Efendi came back.

'*Lailahe illallah*,' he murmured, passing his hands ritually over his face. 'Those Yeriyokush people don't know the meaning of gratitude. They'd stick a knife into the hand that feeds them. Just for a few cheap shoddies . . .'

'Just for a few cheap shoddies . . .' echoed the elders.

The next morning, a little after sunrise, a loud clamour roused the village. Soon the news was all over the place. Jemile Woman's daughter had eloped, and the abductor was someone from Yeriyokush.

'It was plain as a pikestaff,' said one of the elders, 'that the lad meant business when he came in yesterday.'

A couple of hours later, Jemile Woman was seen bearing down on the shop like a thunderclap.

'Filthy-bearded old panderer! You did it, you!'

She heaved a stone at Mehmet Efendi, who closed the door hastily.

'Don't, sister! What are you doing? Why pick on me?'

She raked the ground, raising clouds of dust, and the stones flew at the door.

'You know why, you filthy-bearded old pimp!' she howled, a dishevelled fury, her clothes all torn, her breasts hanging out like a pair of leather pouches.

One of the elders cautiously drew back the door.

'Don't, sister! Why pick on the poor man? What would he get out of your daughter's abduction? The girl had a fire in her loins and she eloped with her lover, that's all . . .'

The woman vanished in a whirl of dust and a huge stone thudded against the wall, missing the old man by inches. He slammed the door shut as quickly as he could.

'The mad bitch! Just because her daughter's got a fire in her loins . . .'

'It's your own daughter who's a bitch,' screeched Jemile Woman. 'And so's your daughter-in-law!'

The old man half-opened the door again.

'Look, sister,' he tried to propitiate her. 'Why don't you go and complain to the Government? There's a Government and there's a law. What do you want of this poor devil?'

The dust churned up again and another stone came hurtling down.

'You don't know his tricks, old man. You don't know! I know. I!'

Mehmet Efendi's hand was on his watch-chain and the watch went bobbing in and out, in and out of his waistcoat-pocket.

'Tell me, Aghas,' he whimpered, 'what's she got on me? A man of my age! Would I ever . . . Such calumny! What's it to do with me if her daughter's eloped?'

One of the boards suddenly split open under the hail of stones. Mehmet Efendi's small eyes almost disappeared into his fleshy face. His thick neck was as red as a turkey's.

'Oh dear, oh dear! What a curse! At my age . . . What can a man do? Ah, my friends, I'll kill myself, I will . . .'

He was twisting this way and that in the dimness of the shop, huge beads of perspiration rolling down his face. His hand shuttled up and down like a machine.

Crack . . .

'The door, Aghas! She's breaking the door . . .'

Sullu, who was sitting in his accustomed place opposite the door, never moved his chin from his stick. Only his hands trembled slightly.

'The door! The door, Efendis! Is it possible? . . . Please, Efendis, please . . .'

'Filthy-bearded . . .'

Crash!

Suddenly Mehmet Efendi's hand stopped dead and his eyes gleamed. He pulled out a length of red calico from the rolls of cotton cloth, measured it mechanically and folded it up. Then he weighed two pounds of sugar into a paper bag. A swarm of flies rose up and settled again on the large gunny sack.

'Rustem Agha,' he said, 'take this and give it to that she-devil or she'll wreck everything, Allah strike her blind!'

Rustem Agha opened the door, but closed it in the nick of time, narrowly escaping a stone.

'Bitch!' he shouted. 'You nearly killed me . . .' In the same breath, he dashed out and seized her by the hair.

'What are you squawking for? Here, take these and go home.'

She flung the offerings off like hot potatoes. The red-flowered calico unfurled in the dust and the sugar lumps scattered here and there.

'Help, neighbours!' she howled. 'Heeeelp! It's a plot. They're all hand in glove with that monster from Darendeh. The old men too. Help!'

Some little girls who were looking on picked up the things and placed them beside her. At last, she slowly drew the calico and the sugar into her apron and turned back home muttering to herself.

They opened the door and a dazzling light poured into the shop. The dust outside was settling. They all stared at the battered door.

'Just look at that whore's handiwork,' they commented. 'It'll take more than fifteen liras to get it repaired.'

The moon had not yet risen and in the darkness of the night the mulberry-tree swayed, vague and huge, like some black spectre. Suddenly, the villagers, who had gathered on the bank of the stream where it was cool, saw a narrow flame spurt up from under the mulberry-tree and start licking away at its branches. In an instant the whole tree was aglow.

A long shrill cry rent the air.

'Fiiire!'

They all rushed up helter-skelter. The shop was burning and Mehmet Efendi was dancing up and down in a frenzy, his hand working away furiously at his chain. His small eyes had sunk well into his flesh and his fat red nape shone even redder in the light of the flames. He kept up a strident yelling.

'Help, good people! I'm lost . . . Quick, people, hurry!

I'm ruined. My children ... Hungry ... All these years in this village ... And now ... Help!'

The villagers set to work with buckets of water, wet rags and earth, and soon had the fire in hand. Then, tired and sweating, they all squatted down before the shop while Mehmet Efendi ran around kissing everyone's hand in turn.

'You've rescued me ... You've saved my life! My family ... Allah!'

'It's that brat did it,' declared Toss Osman. 'Find him now if you can, the tongueless son-of-a-bitch!'

'What's it got to do with him if Jemile's daughter has been carried off?' exclaimed another. 'But try and make a madman see sense!'

'He's not mad or anything,' objected a quavering voice. 'It's a smart fellow's handiwork, this!'

'But he'll wreak mischief on this village yet,' protested someone.

'He'll be a trouble-maker when he grows up,' agreed another.

'That he will,' cried Toss Osman, springing up excitedly. 'Don't you remember what he did to Haji Yusuf last year? Is it possible, I ask you? All Haji Yusuf said to him was: "Bring me a glass of water." And Sullu never moved, did not even open his mouth! "Get me some water, will you!" But sooner an answer from the grave than from that fiend. So Haji Yusuf lost his temper and boxed his ears. Would you believe it? It was as if he hadn't even touched him! Sullu never turned a hair. And the next morning, when Haji came to his field, what should he see? The whole five acres of water-melons nipped at the roots! The boy had gone through the lot with a knife, never missing a stalk!'

'There's no reforming the likes of him. He'll go from bad to worse ...'

'Haji collared him and beat him till he was tired. Then he tied him by the feet to the big mulberry-tree at Skyridge and left him hanging there for a whole day. The rope had cut into his ankles and his feet were an ugly black . . . And then, a couple of days later, we saw Haji Yusuf's wheat field ablaze, the flames leaping from sheaf to sheaf. By the time we'd stamped the fire out, half the crop had gone.'

'It's a blessing the boy never thought of waiting until after the wheat had been threshed,' observed someone.

'Haji Yusuf would've gone hungry that winter if he'd thought of that,' agreed Toss Osman. 'But the boy's one year older now . . . I'm ready to cut my head off if there's any person in this village who can find him. If nothing else, he'll slip down some water-well and stay there for three days, without bread, without water . . . He's not afraid of anything, that one!'

The men were drifting away one by one.

'Just wait,' said Mehmet Efendi vengefully. 'He'll set fire to the whole village yet. Today, it's only me . . . Just let him grow up a little and you'll see. He'll grab a box of matches and make a bonfire of all our homes.'

It was still early morning, but Mehmet Efendi had already opened the shop. He flapped a hand and a swarm of flies rose from the groceries. The hand stopped in mid-air. A long thin shadow holding a stick was reaching out to the door. In a second Sullu stood in the doorway. Mehmet Efendi's face blanched as the boy walked into the shop and took up his usual place on the wooden bench opposite the door. His sun-bleached hair stuck out like a hedgehog's quills over his small freckled face. His upper teeth were long and gleamed through the thin line of his lips. In his stern face, only the eyes were blue and soft. Chin on stick, he gazed steadily at the shopkeeper, and the semblance of a smile flitted over his face.

Mehmet Efendi's hand was on his chain and the watch went bobbing, in and out, in and out of his waistcoat-pocket. He looked thoughtfully at the boy. Then, heaving a deep sigh, he filled up a paper bag from a jar of coloured candy, selected a small mirror figuring a naked girl on its back, also a slingshot, a glass marble, a red kerchief and added a one-lira coin. These he took up to Sullu, placing them on the bench beside him. Sullu glanced at the treasures out of the corner of his eye. He picked up the mirror, turned it over this way and that, then put it back on the bench. He rested his chin on his stick again and sat motionless, gazing at the shopkeeper.

'My child!' cried Mehmet Efendi, growing more and more flustered. 'My brave lad, what harm have you ever seen from me? Tell me, tell me, what? Don't you know that Jemile Woman, the slanderous bitch? At my age! . . . Abduct a girl! Really, my child, may I be struck blind if . . . You know I love you like my son. I always have. I love valiant lads like you. Look, my beautiful child, this shop is yours. Come in any time and take what you want. Any time, whether I'm in or not. Take everything, if you like! From now on, you're my very own son, d'you hear? All that belongs to me is yours. Here, let me give you another mirror. See how it flashes bright as electric light? See the lovely girl rising out of the sea? There, take it, my good lad. You're my own son now. And mark my words, I'll marry you off when you're of age. I'll pay for your wedding and all . . .'

Sullu rose and went behind the counter. He selected three more bird slings and put them into the pocket of his white, handwoven shalvar-trousers.

'Take them, my son, take them!' said Mehmet Efendi, grinding his teeth. 'Whatever you want in this shop . . .'

Rustem Agha was the first to arrive, followed by Haji Agha, Toss Osman, Ansha Fahri and the others. They all stopped dead on the threshold, gaping at Sullu sitting calmly on the bench, chin on stick.

After a while, the shopkeeper went out.

Rustem Agha's white beard quivered.

'Look here, you little devil,' he exclaimed, 'what are you up to? D'you want to ruin the poor man? And you're not even ashamed to show yourself here!'

'D'you realize you can go to hell for this,' Haji Agha chimed in, 'and roast in its flames for ever?'

'Allah always punishes evil . . .' pursued Rustem Agha.

'Well, then,' Ansha Fahri broke in tartly, 'it seems Allah's punished Mehmet Efendi! Good for Sullu! The fellow only got what he deserved.'

'Get!' said Rustem Agha angrily. 'You're just being ungrateful, forgetting all we owe him. Shame on you!'

Ansha Fahri, a thin, long, dark-complexioned man with thick red lips, jumped up excitedly and faced Rustem Agha.

'Listen to me, Uncle,' he said. 'It's that scoundrel who's ungrateful. Doesn't he sell his wares to us for twice the price in town. Now, doesn't he?'

'It's credit, my son! Who'd do that for us in the town?'

'Yes, and now we're all as good as share-cropping for him, aren't we? Just figure out what he makes off our backs . . . Is there one of us who doesn't turn over half and more of his earnings to that man? Now, is there?'

'Don't let's be ungrateful, my son . . .'

'There you go again, Uncle, with your cobwebby notions!' cried Fahri impatiently. 'And I say, set a thief to catch a thief. Good for Sullu!'

'You mustn't go egging the child on or the next thing he'll do is set fire to all our houses.'

'No, he won't!' retorted Fahri. 'Only to such crooks as Mehmet Efendi . . .'

Just then the shopkeeper came in. He pretended he had heard nothing.

'Eh, Fahri Efendi, my son,' he began affably, 'your mother dropped in yesterday. What a woman, Allah grant her long life! One doesn't often see the likes of her in this world. An angel from heaven . . . I'd give my right arm to have such a mother. She's both a mother and a father to you . . .'

A thin ragged man burst into the shop.

'I've had enough, Mehmet Efendi!' he shouted. 'Ten years! I give and give and it never ends. Each year I think it's finished and each year at harvest time you open that yellow book of yours and my debt multiplies itself. I've had enough. You'll not get anything more out of me, not even if you bring the Government to help you . . .'

'Get!' cried the shopkeeper. 'That's what comes of doing good! You're treated as a liar, a swindler. Get! Who wants anything of you, my friend?'

He stopped short. A strong voice was calling outside.

'Raisins, kerchiefs! Buy my wares! Mirrors, calicos . . . Cheap, my wares! Cotton, needles . . .'

The pedlar passed before the open door, driving before him two donkeys loaded with showcases.

'Look!' said the ragged man. 'That lad sells for half the price you charge us, you heathen!'

'Kerchiefs! Buy my wares . . . Cheap . . . Easy to buy!'

A young girl glided into the shop.

'Uncle Mehmet,' she said softly, 'you don't happen to have a buckle? With stars on it . . .'

The shopkeeper seemed flustered.

'No, my girl,' he said quickly. 'We haven't any of that kind.'

She walked off, her broad hips swaying under the red dress and the black shalvar-trousers.

Mehmet Efendi waited a while, then went out too.

She had stopped behind a hut and was looking out for him, her eyes lambent under the long lashes.

'Look here, my girl,' said Mehmet Efendi, 'would I ever do anything to harm you? You're like a daughter to me, that's what! Would a man do anything bad to his own daughter? What I'm saying is that a country man is one thing, a town man another. Suppose you take this young Ali. God knows I've got nothing against him. He's a fine lad. But he's poor as a rat. All your life you'll be dragging after him, working yourself to death in the cotton-fields, threshing, carrying loads . . . A peasant's life is a dog's life, my girl. Barefooted, your feet dirty and cracked . . . And before you know it, your beauty has faded away. You're an old hag with a dozen whining brats at your heels, always naked, hungry or sick . . . The townspeople have found a remedy for this. One child, a second one . . . And then a shot. And that's the end of it. No more bothering about babies or anything! Now, this fellow's set his heart on you, a real corporal who can have girls galore in the city just by waving a hand. Are you going to let this chance slip through your fingers? Like a lady you'll be! Ali's all right, worth two corporals, but there's no help for it, he's poor . . . With this corporal, you'll even wear a coat like the town ladies, gloves on your hands, so they shouldn't get chapped, polished shoes on your feet . . . Tell me now, where's the woman in this village who's so much as seen a pair of shoes since the day she was born? You'll be able to wear shoes even at home. But here you won't even get enough bread to eat. In the town, the bread is white. Pure, snow-white bread! A real corporal! Why, my dear, his monthly salary is more than you and Ali can make by slaving a lifetime. You know best, my girl, but this from me is real fatherly advice.'

'But Ali will kill me,' whispered the girl.

'Nonsense, my dear! The corporal will send a couple of gendarmes and summon Ali to the police-station, where they'll give him a good fright. Don't you realize he's the Government? A mighty corporal . . . Are you going to throw this chance away? When you're still young and beautiful . . . Get your bundle ready at once.'

The girl's lips were half-open, her large black eyes thoughtful.

'Easy to buy! Cheap, my kerchiefs!' came the pedlar's voice.

Mehmet Efendi's face blanched. His hand went to his chain.

'And you, do this for me, my girl,' he said. 'Tell the women not to buy from this tramp. His wares are all rotten, just discarded factory goods. That's why they're cheap. The women don't know. Tell them . . .'

Sullu sat motionless on the bench, gazing dreamily at the shopkeeper and Black Duran who were talking in undertones.

Mehmet Efendi waved a hand and a swarm of black flies rose from the groceries, then settled back again.

'Look, Duran, my son,' he said ingratiatingly, 'if you do this for me, I take it upon me to marry you off and pay for the wedding and all. I can't bear this. It's killing me. My honour . . . As for the boys, give them the raisins and sweets. There'll be more for them afterwards.'

Black Duran straightened up, stretching his thin neck.

'All right, uncle,' he said. 'Since it's a question of honour . . . And anyway, he's a stranger. What business has that tramp in our village? You'll see how I'll deal with him!'

'And if I don't have you married this year, my name's not Mehmet! Just show me what you can do.'

All the children under twelve seemed to have gathered on the edge of the clearing before the shop. They were holding stones and their pockets too were crammed full of stones. They were milling about, expectant and raring to go. A fight broke out between two boys, but Black Duran separated them. With his short stature, he looked hardly more than twelve himself. Away from the rest, leaning against the brush wall of a hut, stood Sullu with his stick . . .

'Look sharp, you buggers,' hissed Black Duran. 'Here he comes, the enemy of all honest people.'

The children closed ranks as they sighted the pedlar and the two donkeys with the showcases flashing in the sunlight.

'Cheap, my wares! Kerchiefs, slings for the boys . . . Good, solid wares . . .'

Black Duran raised his right arm.

'Forward,' he shouted. 'March!'

A hail of stones and fresh dung rained upon the unsuspecting pedlar. He shrank down, trying to protect his head. The donkeys huddled against each other, and a crack zigzagged the glass of one of the showcases. Then in one leap Sullu stood before the children. He swung his stick a couple of times. The hail of stones and dung was cut short and the boys scuttled off, dispersing behind the huts. The pedlar looked up. His eyes were startled and grateful. Sullu standing, met his gaze. Then they both looked towards the shop.

Black Duran rushed panting into the shop.

'Uncle,' he said, 'there we were making short work of the tramp, when Sullu butted in and the boys got the wind up. Somehow, that devil has all the children trembling before him. What can I do? The boy's mad. Everyone here knows that. I could give him a sound thrashing, but that wouldn't get us anywhere with him . . .'

'Again!' cried the shopkeeper. 'Allah strike him blind . . . Duran, my son, there's only one thing to be done.' He seized a roll of flowered calico. 'Here, take this to that mad demon's mother. Talk her into getting him out of the village by hook or by crook for a couple of hours. Just two hours will be enough . . . Once he's out of the way, the affair's in the bag . . .'

It was late afternoon and the great mulberry's shadow was stretching long and dark before the shop when Sullu returned from his uncle's field where his mother had sent him on an errand. His heart missed a beat as he caught sight of the two donkeys lying listlessly by the wayside. Then he saw the pedlar squatting against a fence, motionless, his head bowed. The showcases lay on the ground, empty, their glass smashed to shivers, and round about in the dust were scattered pell-mell the sweets, calicos, toys and other wares they had contained.

He stopped before the pedlar, his hands trembling. The man raised his head and looked at him with hurt eyes. His lower lip was cut and blood was clotted all over his head. They gazed at each other. Then Sullu walked towards the shop.

Quietly, ignoring the petrified shopkeeper, he went behind the counter. Half a dozen bird slings, a good assortment of glass marbles, raisins, a couple of pocket torches, kerchiefs . . . Systematically he collected the items and heaped them on a length of calico which he knotted into a huge bundle.

The shopkeeper's face turned from grey to purple, but he never said a word.

When he had finished, Sullu went and planted himself before Mehmet Efendi. He stood there looking at him for some time. Then, suddenly, he spat on him with all his might.

The shopkeeper's face was left spattered with frothy spittle.